SECRETS OF A SUMMER PLACE
SECRETS OF A MUSTANG ISLAND
BOOK ONE

SYLVIA MCDANIEL

VIRTUAL BOOKSELLER

Copyright

Copyright © 2022 Sylvia McDaniel
Published by Virtual Bookseller, LLC
All Rights Reserved
Cover Design: Dar Albert
Edited by Tina Winograd
Release date: August 2022
ebook ISBN 978-1-950858-86-6
Paperback ISBN 978-1-950858-87-3

This book and parts thereof may not be reproduced in any form, stored in a retrieval system, or transmitted in any form by any means—electronic, mechanical, photocopying, or otherwise—without prior written permission of the author and publisher, except as provided by the United States of America copyright law. The only exception is by a reviewer who may quote short excerpts in a review.

❦ Created with Vellum

Jennifer Moss is having a really bad day.... But it's about to get even worse...

Her teenage son's grades have plummeted. Her husband is distant and cold, and now she's received a letter from the child she gave up for adoption twenty-five years ago.

But a knock on the door from the police spins her world out of control.

Having lost everything, she packs up and returns to Mustang Island where the secrets from her past are slowly revealed. And the boy she left behind so many years ago helps her to see that this new beginning could be the best thing that's ever happened to her.

But will their secret child unravel their relationship before it has a chance to begin again?

To Debbie
This is the life I wish you had lived.
Rest in peace.

CHAPTER 1

Hollywood, California

Staring at the envelope in her hand, Jennifer Moss sat in her Volvo waiting to pick up her son from the Hollywood high school baseball practice. Before she left the house, she'd grabbed the mail.

Now, an eerie sense of foreboding spiraled through her and filled her with anxiety. But then every time she received a piece of mail in which she didn't recognize the name on the envelope, her stomach churned.

Could this be from her? How many times had she gotten her hopes up for them only to be dashed? Would this be the same?

A soft breeze blew through the window on the cloudless day. For a moment, she stopped breathing as she stared at the address.

Madison Wilson, Austin, Texas.

Who did she know in Austin? Who was Madison

Wilson? Anytime she received an envelope like this, her heart would pound in her chest and she would wonder if she'd been discovered.

Part of her wanted to be found, but then she would think of her life now. No one knew. It had been her secret for twenty-six years.

The memory of the house on Mustang Island overwhelmed her. She'd never returned after that summer, and since her parents' deaths, the house sat vacant. As much as she loved that place, she'd never go back because she would have to face the past.

A past that was heart wrenching and left her scared and hating her family.

Shouts from the field alerted her that the team would be leaving practice shortly. The coach always ended their practice with a pep rally. The kids were a good team and might make it to state this year. For her son's sake, she hoped so.

With a sigh, she tore open the envelope and pulled out the letter.

My name is Madison Wilson. According to the genealogy report, your DNA and my DNA are linked. It says you're my birth mother. I would like to speak to you and find out why you gave me up for adoption. I would also like to learn my medical background and even see if we have anything in common. If you are willing to speak to me, please contact me at...

A cry escaped her and the memories flooded her of that terrible day. Her name was Madison. Her heart leaped with a joy only a mother could feel.

Madison gave her address, her phone number, and even her email address.

It had taken twenty-five years, but her secret was about to be revealed. With a sigh, she stared out at the baseball field and let the memories of that day overwhelm her. How she had clung desperately to her child until her mother ripped the infant from her arms and gave her to the nurse.

She'd never seen the baby again after that day. Tears filled her eyes and trickled down her face. How many times had she thought of finding her and telling her how much she wanted to keep her? In the end, she thought it better not to disrupt her life and had done her best to move on. Now that child was grown and wondering why she had not been wanted.

But the opposite was true.

Oh, God, how she'd wanted to keep her. To love her and raise her as her own.

That time in her life had been the worst, and she'd never forgiven her mother for forcing her to give up her child for all the right reasons. They were not what Jennifer wanted to hear.

Sometimes doing the right thing was not the easiest. And having that child taken from her arms was gut-wrenching.

Her handsome son walked across the school yard, his head down. Quickly she wiped the tears from her eyes and shoved the letter into her purse.

How was her family going to react to this news?

Her husband Ryan didn't know about her unwed pregnancy and subsequent birth. And her two smart, intelligent, beautiful children had no idea they had a half-sister. This secret had remained hidden for twenty-five years, but no more.

The door opened and her son slid in.

"Hi, Mom," he said and she could see he was upset.

"Bad day?" she asked.

"Kind of," he replied as he looked out the window of the car.

Something had been eating at him and she didn't know what. He refused to talk to her about it, and only said, *I'm okay.* But he wasn't. His grades had gone from honor roll to barely passing and she feared he was going to lose his scholarship to his favorite school.

No matter how she tried to approach him, the walls came slamming down. And today's mail would not make the situation any easier. Yet, she had waited so long for this letter. So long to hear from the baby she loved instantly.

He looked at her and studied her for a moment. "Are you all right?"

"Sure," she said, wondering how he could tell something was up. "Got something in my eye a moment ago."

"Oh," he said and gazed back out the window as she pulled out of the school parking lot.

"Is Dad going to be home tonight?"

"I don't know," she said. "This morning he left early because it's his surgery day."

Alex made a noise she couldn't quite interpret.

Her husband was a leading plastic surgeon in the Hollywood community and had worked on many stars in his practice. The money he brought in had made it easy for her to stay home and raise their two children.

But the hours he worked were sometimes long, and he often came home exhausted. Lately, he seemed to work longer and longer, though he'd promised her he was going to cut back his hours.

In the twenty years they'd been married, she often wondered if she'd traded love for money. Their marriage was good, but they spent so little time together, with him working so many hours. Sometimes it felt like they were two individual people living in the same house.

And there were days she felt lonely. If not for the kids, she would spend her evenings alone. And even they were growing up and moving on with their lives. Taylor would soon finish her second year of college, and next fall, Alex would be going to a university.

"How's the team doing?"

"If we continue to win, we should make the high school playoffs," he said, staring out the window.

Alex was normally so happy and excited and eager to talk, but in the last two months, he'd withdrawn into himself and she couldn't find a way to bring him out. The kid should be so excited about his team making the playoffs, and yet he didn't act like he cared.

Something was eating at her son and she missed the happy-go-lucky young man who was eager to begin his life.

"That's great news," she said. "When's your next game? Maybe me and your dad can both attend."

Ryan had only made it to one game. One, and soon

their son's season and high school career would be at an end. Sometimes she hated Ryan's job, even though their life was luxurious because of his career.

That didn't excite Alex and she knew she had to learn what troubled him.

Sometimes she wished Ryan was an accountant or even a salesman and not a busy doctor.

Maybe after Alex graduated, she would get them reservations at Cozumel and take the kids down to the beach. She doubted that Ryan would take the time off. But it would be good to spend some time with her children.

The thought of Madison crossed her mind and she wondered if she would like to go with them.

"That would be nice," he said. "The next game is Saturday morning."

That was Ryan's tee time. Surely he could give up golfing one Saturday for his son. But nothing came between Ryan and his golf.

They pulled into the drive and the gate opened automatically. She pulled into the back garage. The pool man had been here today, and maybe later tonight, she'd get in the water and swim a few laps.

Closing the garage door, they both exited the car and walked into the house, entering through the laundry room.

"Good afternoon, Mrs. Moss, Alex," the maid said to her. "Dinner is in the oven. I'm leaving for the day."

"Thank you, Esmeralda," she said softly.

Alex walked past the woman and that was so unusual for him. Normally he would hug Esmeralda and tell her the cooking was divine. But not today.

Glancing at her son, Jennifer was worried. Maybe it was time to suggest counseling. Anything to keep his grades from falling even further. Anything to keep him from losing his scholarship. Anything to bring the boy she loved back to her.

"Good night," Esmeralda called as she exited the back door.

Jennifer walked into the massive kitchen and there was a salad sitting out and a casserole ready to turn on in the oven.

"Mom," Alex said, walking back into the kitchen. "Coach said I had to give you this."

She glanced at the envelope he held in his hand.

Taking it, she opened it to the letter inside.

"Damn it, Alex," she said as she read the letter. "What is going on?"

He shrugged. "Don't know."

"If you don't bring your grades up you're going to lose your scholarship. You're about to be kicked off the baseball team. This is not my son. Tell me what is wrong."

With a grimace, he turned and walked out of the kitchen. "Maybe I want to do high school over again. Maybe I'm a loser."

"Alex, don't walk away. Let's sit down and talk about this."

He ignored her and went up the stairs to his room.

Shaking her head, she couldn't wait for Ryan to get home. They had to have a serious talk with Alex, and she had to tell him she had another child. Madison.

Reaching inside the refrigerator, she pulled out a full bottle of wine and poured herself a glass.

It was going to be a hell of a night.

CHAPTER 2

Three hours later, Jennifer sat in the den, trying to watch a silly television show, her mind scattering from one child to the next. This evening, she tried to call Taylor, needing to hear the sound of her sweet voice. But she was a college kid and she must have been out with friends.

After calling her twice, she gave up.

She was so worried about Alex and couldn't wait to speak to Ryan about their son. It was time to consider getting professional help for him. Her star pupil's grades had reached bottom and his bubbly personality seemed to have died. What had happened to bring about this drastic change in him?

And no matter how hard she tried to reach him, she hit a wall.

Now there was Madison, and she didn't know how her husband and children were going to accept the news that she had given up a baby for adoption. After her mother took the baby from her arms, she'd done her best to try to keep the memory of her locked away. It was the only way she learned that she could keep the hurt from overwhelming her. And yet, not a day had gone by that she hadn't wondered about what she looked like and if she had a happy life.

Tonight, the house felt so empty and she feared what it would be like when Alex went to college. The place was like a tomb as she walked from room to room, pacing, worrying, thinking about the child she gave up and speculating when her husband would get home.

As she wandered through the house, she couldn't help but think how lonely it felt. Was this what her life would always be like? Her children in college, her husband at his job?

Tonight Ryan was later than ever. Normally, he walked in around eight at the very latest. Oftentimes, she'd wondered if he was really at the clinic or was he languishing in the arms of some woman. But then she would tell herself that she was being paranoid.

She had no reason to suspect her husband of cheating. None. His only mistress was his dedication to his profession. His patients.

Around seven, she gave up on him and cooked the casserole. Together, she and Alex sat at the table alone. The bright, bubbly boy of the past sat glumly and ate his dinner, seldom speaking. She'd tried to talk to him again about his grades, but it was like a wall had come down and she'd finally given up.

Did he want to fail?

Maybe when Ryan got home, he could reach their son. But Alex wasn't talking to her. Would he talk to his father?

Now sitting here in her favorite chair, the letter sat like a stone on her chest while the television rambled on, without her really seeing or hearing the noise.

What would this child look like? Would she have her hair and eye coloring or her father's? And where was her father? At twenty-five, her first daughter must be out of college. What had she done with her life?

Pain gripped Jennifer's chest at the thought of all she'd missed out on Madison's life. Her first steps, her first words, the cuddles and hugs. Her first dance recital, her first day of school.

Tears welled in her eyes and she got up and paced the floor.

Had her childhood been a great one? Did her adoptive parents give her the love she deserved? Would she hate Jennifer for giving her up?

While she knew her mother had been right to force her to give up the baby for adoption, it had been the hardest thing she'd ever done. And in her mind, she'd searched for some way to keep her. But being a mother at seventeen with no education would have guaranteed they would have struggled. Jennifer had been willing to make that sacrifice. She would have chosen the baby over her abundant life, but her mother had not given her that option.

And neither had Dylan, the boy she had loved and waited for day after day.

After her mother demanded that she give the child up, their relationship had never been the same. In many ways,

Jennifer hated her mother and the way she had erased all the memories from that time from their family. It was like those nine months never happened, but they had.

There were no photos of Jennifer pregnant, nothing to show that time ever occurred. No photos of the baby. And yet a young life walked the earth because of Jennifer and Dylan. A young life that she never wanted to give up.

And the father of that child had been a huge disappointment. After the night of the party, they had spent every day together until her parents suspected her pregnancy and they left the island.

Early one morning, her parents packed up their summer home and returned to Dallas, leaving Jennifer's heart out near a sand dune. Though she'd called him multiple times, he'd never returned her calls or her letters.

Dylan's face appeared in her memory and she wondered what he looked like now. Was he happy? Had he ever thought of her again? But she would never know because she would not search him out. If he could walk away from her, then she didn't want to ever see him again.

Pacing the floor, she knew that life was about to change and she worried how her family would accept the news of her first daughter. No matter what they thought, she would welcome her child with open arms. So many years had passed since she'd seen her and she didn't want to waste any more time.

Tonight she would tell Ryan about Madison. Tonight everything would be revealed.

The doorbell rang. It was late. Who could be coming to see them at this time of night? She grabbed her phone and looked at the security app. Two policemen stood at the door.

Why were they here?

What if it was about Taylor? Could that be why she hadn't been able to reach her tonight?

She ran to the door, fear clutching her heart, feeling like she was in a dream. She could not face losing one of her children, ever. She'd lost one, she refused to lose another.

When she opened the door, they stared at her.

"Mrs. Moss?"

"Yes," she said, knowing instinctively from their expressions they were not delivering good news.

The man seemed to gather his courage as he took a deep breath. "We regret to inform you that your husband died of a heart attack this evening at his clinic."

"Ryan?" she said, a surreal feeling overcoming her. "Dr. Ryan Moss?"

"Yes, ma'am," the man said. "Do you have someone here with you?"

Ryan was dead. Her husband was dead.

"My son," she said. Oh my God, she would have to tell her children their father was dead.

"Alex," she cried, the slow realization that Ryan would never come home again hitting her as tears filled her eyes. No, their marriage had not been perfect, but still, she loved him.

Shock seemed to cushion her as the words reverberated through her mind. Ryan was dead. Her husband was dead.

All night, she'd been waiting for him to come home and he was dead. Dead. Ryan was dead.

Grief hit her like a tsunami wave knocking her to her knees. No more quick kisses in the morning. No more rushing out the door, barely acknowledging her. No more hugs in the night.

"Ma'am, are you all right?" the policeman asked.

No, she wasn't all right. Her world had exploded around her. Nothing would ever be the same after this day. The good news about Madison and the death of her husband were all delivered with a bang in one day.

"What's wrong, Mom," Alex said, coming up behind her. He pulled her up from the ground and gazed at the police officers.

"Your father died of a heart attack tonight," she said, throwing her arms around him and sobbing on his shoulder. "Ryan is dead."

CHAPTER 3

Jennifer sat in a chair on the front row of the graveside and gazed at the coffin. Her son sat on one side of her and her daughter on the other. Numb, she barely blinked while the preacher said his final words.

A cool breeze blew and the smell of the flowers piled on the casket and the many wreaths filled the air.

It was over. She was a widow. No more kisses. No more hugs. No more long stares at her like he couldn't understand what she was saying, like his genius brain didn't accept the obvious.

Ryan never walked anywhere but ran. Now he was running in heaven and even probably doing surgery there. Someone must need a facelift in heaven.

All of his office staff attended the service, neighbors, his golfing friends, her ladies' club members, and even a few family members. They were all here, and yet as she stared at the coffin, she'd never felt more alone.

It didn't seem real.

Alex had not shed a single tear, but moved about woodenly like he feared at any moment he would break. Her daughter was taking her father's death especially hard and she gripped her hand in hers. Jennifer had cried until there were no tears left, but it still didn't feel real.

Any moment, she expected him to walk up and ask why everyone was so sad. *I'm right here. This has been a huge misunderstanding.*

But it was real. In the last two days, she'd had to deal with getting his body from the morgue to the funeral home. Contacting his family and telling them he was gone. His parents were deceased, but he had brothers and sisters, nieces and nephews, and many were sitting behind her.

Planning his funeral had been the most difficult thing she'd ever done. Not even her parents had been this hard. But how did you memorialize someone who was such a brilliant man? The church had been filled with well-known doctors who had operated with him or sent him patients.

The day felt surreal. But the sky was a dazzling blue and the California sun shone brightly on them.

They said the final prayer and she couldn't bow her head. All she could do was stare at the box that held his body. These were their final moments together and she sat trying to remember what he said to her that morning before he left. That final good-bye that neither one of them knew would be the end.

How could she know that would be the last time she'd see him?

The funeral director bent over to her. "Ma'am, the car is waiting for you whenever you're ready to leave. No hurry."

"Thank you," she heard herself say as she sat there wondering what was next.

Friends and family walked by and told her how sorry they were. And all she could do was nod and whisper *thank you*.

"Ma'am," Fiona Brown, his nurse from the office leaned down and took her hand, "I know this is a difficult time and I'm so sorry for your loss. We all loved Dr. Moss. But there are some things at the office that need to be taken care of right away. I'm sorry to tell you this, but the staff has not been paid in almost a month."

Jennifer jerked her head up and gazed at Fiona. "Really? Why not?"

Fiona shrugged. "I don't know, but some of them are starting to get really anxious about needing their pay."

What happened? Had Ryan known his employees were not being paid.

"Of course," she said, wondering why his bookkeeper had not paid his staff. "Give me just a few days and then I'll come in and take care of it."

She knew that the next few weeks were going to be so difficult straightening out their affairs. Changing everything from two people to one from their bank account to the mortgage, just everything.

After everyone had come by to pay their respects, she watched as people strolled off leaving her and the children alone.

Slowly they rose and walked to the casket still sitting on

the rails. Staring down at the box that held his remains, she felt a chill race up her spine. This was it. Their final good-bye.

"I can't believe he's gone," her daughter said through her tears.

"Me either," Jennifer said. "Mourning him doesn't end today. The hardest part is yet to come."

She wrapped her arms around her children and they stared at the casket. Her son had been quiet for the last three days, saying very little. It almost seemed like he was angry and she didn't know how to reach him.

"Good-bye, Ryan," she said softly. "Rest in peace."

"Bye, Daddy," her daughter said.

Her son pulled away and walked toward the limo waiting for them.

"What's wrong with Alex," her daughter asked.

"I don't know," she said honestly. "Some people handle grief differently."

They turned and began to walk to the car. Her daughter said, "Last night, he got so angry with me when I asked him about Daddy."

Could something have happened between him and Ryan that was causing him to act out? After this weekend, when everything got back to a somewhat normal routine, she was going to ask him to see a counselor.

Tell the counselor what was eating him if he could not tell her. All she wanted was her cheerful son to return.

Somehow she had to reach him and help him get over whatever was troubling him. And now he had to deal with losing his father as well. It just didn't seem fair.

Her husband's employees were standing off to the side talking earnestly amongst themselves. One of the women gave a little laugh and shook her head.

They were just about to get into the limo. Alex stood holding the door open for them when Lily, her neighbor, and her son Kyle approached her.

"Jennifer, I just wanted to tell you how sorry I was about Dr. Moss. He was such a great man and I just don't know how we're going to do without him."

Alex tensed and she could see him looking at Kyle. He mouthed the words *get her out of here.*

His face was red, and at any moment, she feared he was going to explode with fury. What was going on? Why was Alex acting this way?

"Come on, Mom, they need to go," Kyle said, taking her by the arm.

"If you need anything at all, please call me," Lily said. "I'm here for you."

"Thank you," Jennifer said.

Had Kyle and Alex gotten into a disagreement? They had been best of friends since they were in junior high. Come to think of it, she'd not seen Kyle at the house in ages.

Lily and Kyle walked away and Jennifer stood by the door of the limo and gazed at the people still at the cemetery. The office workers were still huddled together and she could tell they were frustrated.

Fiona rolled her eyes at Lily, and Jennifer couldn't help but think that was odd. She knew Lily was a patient because Ryan often made fun of the woman's requests.

She'd had her boobs done twice, her nose, cheek implants, and even a tummy tuck.

He often called her plastic Barbie, but she kept coming in. The latest was a facelift.

But it was over. No one else would receive any help from Dr. Moss's hands. Now Jennifer had to go home, comfort her children, and start filing the necessary paperwork that dissolved everything they owned together.

"Come on, let's go home," she told Taylor and Alex. "Your father's family will be there and all that food that was sent in. Tomorrow it will be just the three of us. But today, we have family to entertain."

And she didn't feel like entertaining anyone.

"Mom, finals are next week. I need to go back to college day after tomorrow," Taylor said.

Jennifer felt her heart clench. She wasn't ready to part with her kids. Not yet. She needed them by her side.

"I understand," she said, softly knowing she had to let her go. They had to get on with their lives, but it seemed so quick. They had not had any time to adjust.

"Don't forget after finals, I'm going to London to study," she said. "Then I'll be home, but Daddy won't be here."

"No, he won't," Jennifer said. "Now we must learn to live without him."

Alex made a harrumph sound. Had he been angry at his father? Could that be what was troubling him? And what did Kyle have to do with the rage that seemed to be seeping from Alex?

CHAPTER 4

*E*arly Monday morning, Jennifer dropped Taylor off at the airport to return to college.

"You're sure you're ready to go back," she said, wondering how one returns to normal after their husband or father dies. It had been five days since the police showed up at her door.

Five days of putting together a funeral, contacting Ryan's family, and supporting her children as they grappled with the death of their father. There had been no time for Jennifer to really process she was now alone.

It felt like an avalanche was roaring toward her where she could only curl into a ball and try not to suffocate.

"You can always stay home and repeat the semester."

While she knew that was impractical, part of her needed her daughter close to her. This was a time she'd have to learn to live without her husband. Her family seemed to be splintering and she couldn't lose her children.

Taylor hugged her. "I can't, Mom. I want to finish this

semester. Plus, I have that trip planned to go to England to study for a month."

Her daughter's minor was British literature and there was a school-sponsored trip to London. At the time they planned it, it seemed like a wonderful idea. Now it was all Jennifer could do not to beg her to postpone the trip or cancel it altogether. But she wouldn't do that.

Life had to go on.

Until now, Jennifer had forgotten all about the trip and knew Taylor was looking forward to going. Her daughter wouldn't be home until mid-to-late June. That seemed like forever.

"Please stay in touch," she told her daughter hugging her close.

"I will," she said. "And if it all becomes too much, I'll come home."

"I love you," Jennifer said, feeling the tears well in her eyes.

"I know. I love you," Taylor said and hurriedly pulled back and got out of the car. "I'll call you when I get back to school."

Jennifer turned her head and wiped the tears. "Safe travels."

Her daughter hurried to the airport doors and disappeared inside. A hole seemed to expand in Jennifer's heart. She loved her children so much and now they were her everything.

Life went on, even after someone important died.

She put the car in gear and started toward the clinic. It bothered her all weekend that Ryan's employees were not getting paid. She'd asked Alex if he wanted to go to his father's office with her and he said no. He was returning to school full-time. He had baseball practice this afternoon.

Her children were moving on with their lives, and while she was glad, she felt like a floundering fish left on shore.

In some ways, Ryan had taken care of everything, and now she had to learn how to take care of their finances, their bills, and all the legal stuff.

Jennifer wove her Volvo through the downtown Los Angeles traffic. It had been so long since she'd driven the freeway this early in the morning that she'd forgotten about the traffic LA was known for.

And after today, she didn't ever want to endure it again if possible.

Finally, a little after nine, she pulled into the parking lot of her husband's clinic. The building was owned by a corporation and he paid them monthly rent. Grabbing her water and a bag for anything she needed to pack up and bring home, she walked toward his office.

Knowing that this was going to be a difficult day, she took a deep breath and entered the building.

Going through the door, she noted there were probably ten offices in the building. She found his and walked inside. Several of the employees were there, packing things and answering the phone.

It was an eerie atmosphere and she instantly hated being there. But she had to deal with closing his office forever.

Fiona came to her. "Good morning. How are you?"

She shrugged. How did you answer that question? No one wanted to hear how she'd cried herself to sleep or that she kept waking up and reaching out for Ryan, but he wasn't there.

"Things will get better, eventually," she said. "Where should I start?"

"Bookkeeping," Fiona said.

"What happened to his bookkeeper, Olivia?"

Fiona shook her head. "He fired her a month ago. Claimed she was stealing. The woman was as honest as they come. She didn't take a dime."

Why had he not said anything to her about Olivia stealing? You would think it would have been something he mentioned to her. He'd seemed so remote lately and now she would never understand what was wrong with him.

Jennifer had taken accounting in college and had a good idea of how business books should look.

"How do we go about closing his office," Jennifer asked.

"We've canceled all of his appointments and we're in the process of writing a letter to his clients that we'd like you to approve."

There had been a big write-up in the paper, but many of his patients probably didn't know that he was gone.

"Are there any drugs in the office?" she asked, knowing that thieves would see he was dead and try to get into his office and steal whatever was left.

"We kept very few on hand and the police confiscated all of them while they were here," she said.

"Good," Jennifer thought. At least if they broke in, there was nothing for them to steal and end up on the street.

"What about the equipment?"

"Sell it," Fiona said. "I've already contacted a company that buys used medical office furniture and equipment. I thought you could use the cash," she said.

Why would Jennifer need the cash?

A frown appeared between her eyes. "Good job. I'm going to need your help with so much."

The woman nodded.

"Here is the login for the computer. This is Dr. Moss's login. Oh, and you'll probably need to go through his office and get everything out of there."

Jennifer had the oddest thought pop into her brain. "Fiona, where did he die?"

The woman blinked her eyes and licked her lips nervously. "He was with a patient in room three."

"He just fell over dead?"

"No, ma'am," she said. "He was examining Mrs. Lily Jackson when the attack occurred."

Lily of all people and the woman had not even mentioned that he died while he examined her. It seemed odd.

"Were you in there with him?"

"Oh no, ma'am," she said, backing toward the door like she wanted to run.

Why wasn't she in there with her husband while he was examining a patient?

"I thought you had to be in there with him while he examined a patient."

"Yes, ma'am," she said. "But he sent us out of the room to talk privately with her."

That still didn't seem right. Lily Jackson was a walking sexpot. All the time, he made fun of their neighbor for the surgeries she wanted done. Often, Jennifer had wondered where she got the money for such expensive elective surgeries.

With a sigh, Jennifer shook her head. "All right, I'm going to get started."

The sooner she began, the sooner she could escape back to her world.

Three hours later, panic was starting to build inside Jennifer. She'd downloaded the latest bank statement for the clinic and was shocked at how much money came in. But even more, how much was going out.

Her husband's clinic should be so far in the green that he could give every employee a huge raise, but instead it showed that the rent was past due, the rental equipment payments were past due, taxes had not been paid, and that the account was almost empty.

So what had Ryan done with all his earnings? Where was the money?

For years, he had insisted on handling their finances and she'd agreed to let him. After all, he had a bookkeeper who worked on the accounts; she didn't need to be involved.

And now Jennifer was starting to feel terrified.

There was a stack of unopened envelopes on the desk and she began to open them one by one. Credit card balances were almost maxed out. One said Final Notice. There was a letter from the state saying that if he didn't pay his employees' federal tax they would close his office. He had until next week to get it filed.

Fiona came to the door. "Are you all right?"

She'd looked at the charges on the credit card statements. Hotels, trips, fancy restaurants, places that he'd never taken her. She had to know.

"Was he having an affair, Fiona?"

The nurse's face blanched and she could see that she didn't want to tell her. But somehow, this felt like he had been cheating on her. From the credit card evidence, he was having a good time with someone other than her.

"Yes, ma'am," she said. "I'm so sorry."

Jennifer released her pent-up breath. This was why he barely had time for her. There had been someone else in his life that he'd been sharing his time and money with. Someone else that he'd been taking to hotels and restaurants and charting private planes to fly to exotic locations with.

Someone else instead of her.

If he wasn't already dead, she would have made sure he was looking six feet up after she cleaned up this mess. But what about their personal accounts. If he'd left his business in this kind of shape, what had he done to their personal life?

What did she not know about that was looming in her future?

"Who was it?"

"A patient," Fiona said. "Someone you know. Because of HIPPA laws, I'm afraid to say much."

Suddenly, the image of Alex tensing as Lily Jackson and

her son Kyle stepped over to the limo the day of the funeral seemed to tease her. Kyle and Alex had barely spoken, but Alex told him to *get her out of there*. Fiona had rolled her eyes at Lily.

Could Ryan have been having an affair with Lily?

Could this be what was troubling her son?

Jennifer stood. "Tell the employees they will be paid. I'll find the money somewhere. In the meantime, would you please start closing this office down? I'm surprised they haven't run him out of here. He was two months behind on the rent."

The woman sighed and shook her head, her face had a pained expression on it.

"This morning, the office manager came down and told me we had one week and then they were going to confiscate everything in here," she said. "I was waiting for you to learn the truth before I said anything."

Shutting down the computer, Jennifer realized she was going to have to move quickly. She opened the drawers of the desk and pulled out their personal documentation. Their home loan, car loans, credit card payments. Everything she needed. Tonight, she would spend time going through and finding out what they owed.

One moment she was missing Ryan, and now, she could feel her anger and her hatred building inside her. The man had cheated on her and she thought she knew with whom.

If he didn't want to stay married, all he had to do was ask for a divorce, but instead he took the coward's way out.

"Thank you for being patient with me. I'll be back first thing in the morning to continue seeing what kind of havoc he created." Grabbing her stuff, she stopped. "Did I miss something that was going on with Ryan? Was it a midlife crisis? At home, he seemed perfectly fine, though I must admit these last few months, he's been gone a lot."

The woman sighed.

"Ma'am, I've worked for him for many years. About the time he bought that sporty Porsche, he changed. It was like he was trying to live like a young man. Not one who was fifty."

Shaking her head, she tried to keep the tears from flowing, but one slipped down her cheek. "Now, I don't know whether to be sad he's gone or to hate him. At the moment, hate is really filling me. How could I not have known?"

All this time, he'd been having an affair and she'd been at home playing the good wife.

The nurse nodded. "Go home and try to rest."

She was going home, but first, she was going to confront her son. She felt he knew about this. And if she could control her temper, she was going to confront that sexpot that lived down the street. Maybe she'd tell her that his autopsy showed he had herpes. Or even worse, Aids.

Most definitely she would tell her to get checked.

CHAPTER 5

Jennifer walked into the house and felt a sense of emptiness fill her. She'd thought they were happy. She'd believed that he loved her and yet he'd been cheating with the woman he made fun of that lived down the street.

How many other women had there been? Did she even want to know?

And what kind of damage had he done to their personal finances? From the appearance of the money statements at his office, he'd been spending like a rock star.

With a sigh, she set her things on the counter and then headed up the stairs. She had to speak to Alex.

With a sigh, she took a deep breath and knocked on his door. He opened it and gazed at her.

"We need to talk," she said.

Without him inviting her, she pushed open the door, walked in, and took a seat on the bed. How did you ask your son if he knew about his father's cheating?

"Since January, you've been acting strange. My happy young man who made me laugh at life has not been the same. At the funeral, I noticed you mouthed to Kyle to 'get her out of here.' You were referring to his mother. Then today while I was at your father's office, I discovered some things that were quite disturbing about Ryan. I think you know what they are," she said softly. "Tell me what you know."

A frown appeared on his face and he glanced away. Tears appeared in the corners of his eyes and her heart ached for him.

"I hate Dad," he said softly. "He's not who I thought he was."

While she didn't want him to hate his father, she also understood. Maybe there would come a day when they both could accept him for who he was, but that wasn't going to be today.

"What did you learn about your father that makes you hate him?"

A tear trickled down his cheek. "No, don't make me say it, Mom. It will hurt you. He's such an ass."

She sighed and stared at this boy she loved so very much. "I'm already hurt. I've gone from grieving your father to wanting to kick his butt. And I'm still learning about the things he's done. But in order to heal, we have to confront this head on. Tell me what happened to make my son withdraw and his grades to plummet. Tell me why you hate him."

His bottom lip trembled and he sighed. His eyes refused to meet hers.

"Kyle and I caught his mother and Dad having sex in the living room. We came home early and they were on the couch doing it. After we caught them, he acted like it was no big deal. Later Dad told me that men keep secrets from their wives." He shook his head and she could see he was still angry. "I thought we were one big happy family. I thought he loved you. He made our life a mockery and a sham. And I hate him for what he did. I hate him for cheating on you."

Pain unlike anything she'd ever felt filled her as she reached over and pulled Alex into her arms. "You're not the only one. I thought so too. But obviously he wasn't happy or I don't know. He never complained about our marriage. I had no idea. But something was wrong."

That wasn't exactly true. Now that she looked back over the last year, he'd stopped spending time with them. He was either at work or out on the golf course. Or maybe he spent that time in some woman's arms.

"If he wanted a divorce, I would have given it to him," she said softly. "If I'd known, I would have kicked him out. Maybe that's what he feared. I don't know."

They sat on the bed, holding each other, crying because they felt so betrayed by the man they obviously didn't know.

"I don't think he wanted a divorce. I think he just wanted to screw women. I'm so sorry, Mom, I should have come and told you, but I didn't want to upset you. And I think there were others besides Lily."

"Oh, son," she said, thinking about how they had sex

once a week and it was a quick tumble that never lasted long. Probably because he'd been doing the nasty with someone else that week.

They pulled apart and she wiped the tears from her eyes.

"This is not your fault. You can't let your father's actions destroy your life. Now, I understand why you were angry. Now I understand why you withdrew from me. Please don't ever do that again. Come and talk to me."

Her son clenched his fists. "He wanted me to pretend that nothing was wrong. That our family life was good while he was out screwing our neighbor and God knows who else. It was all a big lie, and I couldn't stand that you didn't know and Kyle and I went along with the pretense of being happy."

"Does Taylor know?"

"I don't think so, but he was hitting pretty hard on one of her friend's mother. A single lady."

Had everyone known that her husband was a cheater but her? Damn him. Damn him for how he'd hurt their children. And her. Damn him for making her feel like such a fool.

"Are you going to tell her?"

They both needed to know the truth, but right now, she was still uncovering so much of what Ryan had done. Before she made any accusations, she wanted to know everything.

"Today at his office, I discovered that a lot of our life is not how I thought it was, but I don't want to say anything until I get all my facts straight. But soon, we'll hold a family meeting and then I'll tell you what I've learned about your father."

Her son almost growled, the sound was pure hate.

"He spent all the money, didn't he," Alex said, gazing at her, his eyes darkening with anger.

"I don't know yet," she said. "A lot went out. Seems like he had such a great hidden life I knew nothing about."

Shaking his head, his fists gripped together.

"Mom, I think he was paying Kyle's mother's house payment. I'm not certain, but something was said one evening when I was over at Kyle's that later made me think he was. I couldn't stand going over there any longer. I couldn't stand being with Kyle when we both knew what my father was doing to you."

Rage filled Jennifer and she took a deep breath. "Well, wasn't that awfully nice of him. I'll soon find out. I should have realized that something was wrong when you and Kyle were no longer hanging out together."

All the grief she'd felt days ago was slowly transforming into rage and hate. But she had to keep her focus on her son. He was the one his father had hurt the most. He was her priority. That and finding out what, if any, money they had left.

"Alex, if you need to speak to a counselor. If you need help in sorting out this awful mess, please let me know."

A tear trickled down her son's cheek and it was the first time she'd seen him cry. "Mom, it was you I was so worried about. I didn't want him to hurt you. When I learned he was cheating on you, I began to hate him. Remember how he made such a big deal about grades. I didn't want to get good grades because then he was happy. By failing, I knew it would make him angry. I wanted him to be as angry as I felt."

Oh, God, it had been right there in her face and she hadn't seen what was going on. Had she been living under a rock? How could she have missed that her husband was cheating on her? Destroying her son.

"I'm sorry I didn't realize sooner what was going on," she said. "But your grades affect your future. Don't let your anger at him ruin your life. Do better."

Her son reached out and grabbed her and gave her the sweetest hug. "I'm so glad I no longer have to pretend. It was so hard to keep the ugly truth from you. And I hated him so much."

She felt like she'd failed her son. She should have known.

"You can always come and talk to me about anything," she said. "I'm not perfect. I've screwed up many areas of my life, but we can always talk and try to figure out something together."

Alex kissed her on the cheek. It was the first one she'd received from him in a long time.

"Love you," he said.

"Love you," she replied. "You have school tomorrow, so try to get some rest."

"I will," he said smiling.

It was the first smile she'd seen in months and relief filled her. Maybe by clearing the air, she'd get her son back.

Slowly she stood and walked to the door. "Good night, son."

"Good night, Mom," he said and it sounded once again like the boy she knew.

Damn Ryan for what he'd done to their son. Damn him for what he'd done to her.

CHAPTER 6

It was almost midnight. She'd gone through their financial statements, the bank accounts, the loans, everything. The son of a bitch had spent almost every dime of their money. Every dime of their retirement. Every dime of every cent he'd ever earned.

They were basically broke. Even the life insurance policy, he'd cashed it in. She'd been so stupid to let him pay for everything. To give him full control. To not keep watch over their finances, but to believe him.

The one thing he could not touch was the college funds and those were still intact. At least their children could go to school.

And Alex was correct. He had paid not only their mortgage but Lily's as well. In fact, it appeared he bought the house for her and moved her in. That just might work to her advantage. Not one, but two homes in Beverly Hills to sell.

Rage unlike anything she'd ever felt before consumed

her. His damn mistress was living two doors down. Right under her nose. Two doors down, so they could play.

Without thinking, she marched down the street to Lily's house. Yes, it was late, but she didn't care. The woman had stolen a lot from her.

Kyle opened the door. "Mrs. Moss, it's not a good time."

"The hell it isn't," she said and pushed past him into their house.

"Lily, get your ass down here, we need to talk," she screamed.

Just then the woman came around the upstairs corner in a slinky nightgown carrying a bottle of wine. Seemed she'd been drowning her sorrows in alcohol.

Kyle shook his head and disappeared back up to his room.

"Why Jennifer, what brings you here so late," she slurred.

The woman was obviously drunk.

"My dead husband," she said. "You were fucking my dead husband."

Lily giggled and that just incensed her more. "Yes, he died with his penis inside me."

Stunned, Jennifer took a step back. "What?"

Lily's plastic face twisted up as she began to ugly cry. "We were having sex in the patient exam room. He liked to do it there. I was spread out on the exam table. He was pumping into me and suddenly he cried out and grabbed his chest. Then he fell on top of me. I couldn't move. He was still inside me when the paramedics arrived. They had to lift him off me."

Tears rolled down her face. "He was dead when they removed him from me. Dead."

Suddenly Jennifer began to laugh hysterically. After everything she'd been through, this topped it all. The man and woman got what they deserved.

Lily was still ugly crying while Jennifer howled with laughter. She knew she must sound crazy, but she didn't care. The last twenty-four hours had proven to her that her husband was not who she thought he was.

And to think she'd given him a huge Hollywood funeral when they were broke. Son of a bitch.

"He bought you your house and made the house payment?"

"Yes," she said crying "We're going to have to move. I can't pay for this house."

"He paid your utilities and even bought you a car?"

"Yes," she said blubbering harder. "Ryan was very generous to me as long as I…"

The thought made Jennifer nauseous. It was bad enough that he died inside Lily, but to think he expected her to perform was more than she could handle.

"Don't tell me, I don't want to know," Jennifer said. "But be warned that I'm going after your house, your car, everything. Tomorrow morning, I will be speaking to an attorney and we'll be figuring out how best to handle the estate. The money for you should have gone to my children. You and Ryan went through it all."

Lily's bottom lip trembled.

"Just tell me one thing, how long did this affair last?"

"Five years," Lily said. "We met at a medical convention and then he convinced me to move down the street."

How had she been so stupid not to see his deception? Five years, they had carried on without her knowledge.

Oh God, Jennifer felt like someone had just put her in a really bad movie. One that had the audience crying. She wanted to make Lily pay for what she'd done. She wanted her to feel as bad as Jennifer felt right now.

"He used to make fun of you. Of all the different surgeries you wanted done," Jennifer said.

"That was to throw you off. Anytime he thought you were getting suspicious," she said.

And she'd never been suspicious. Damn him. She'd been too stupid to catch on.

"Alex told me he caught the two of you together," she said.

Lily sighed and glanced around to see if her son was in the room. "He and Kyle came home early. They got into a fight over what was going on and have not been friends since."

"You have no shame," Jennifer said. "But then again, Ryan didn't either. It now seems fitting that he died with his penis stuck up your…"

She couldn't say the words. They were gross and demeaning just like her husband and Lily.

"You might want to get checked. The autopsy showed he had Aids."

"What?" Lily said, her eyes widening. "I don't believe you. You're lying."

"You weren't the only one he was sleeping with," she said, knowing it was mean but unable to stop herself.

The woman's mouth opened wide in surprise.

"You'll be hearing from my lawyer," Jennifer said and walked out the door.

The stroll home was not near long enough and she walked the neighborhood. It was a gated community and she felt safe and the night air seemed to clear so much of the anger and hate from her mind.

How had she been so stupid? Now looking back, she realized all the birthdays, the anniversaries, the special occasions he'd missed. She'd believed his patients needed him. Instead, it was so he could play with Lily. And the woman lived only two doors from them.

Right under her nose, he'd kept his little paramour.

Damn him! Damn him!

Walking back to the house, she went inside, sank down on the couch, and cried herself to sleep.

CHAPTER 7

A month later, Jennifer parked her husband's Porsche near his grave, grabbed the bottle of champagne they had saved for their twenty-fifth wedding anniversary, and walked to the grave.

Time to celebrate.

The house was sold, Lily's home was sold, most of the furniture, even her Volvo. The only thing she'd keep was Ryan's convertible Porsche. Just what a single woman needed. Especially one with a grudge.

After walking across the grass, she stopped at his grave. Hard to believe he'd been dead for a month and yet she didn't even miss him. Nothing was the same and she was glad.

"Well, Ryan, Dr. Plastic Dick, this is good-bye," she said. "You son of a bitch, you really screwed me over. Don't worry, I hired an attorney and got your financial mess straightened out. Your employees are paid, the clinic is closed, our house is sold, and even your sweet paramour's house that you bought has sold."

She laughed. "I've learned that I can be a real mean bitch. So yes, I kicked her to the curb. You should have taken better care of her. Now she's searching for another rich man to satisfy with her well-built body. You did a good job making her beautiful. I'm sure she'll find someone very soon."

The breeze blew through the cemetery and she worked the cork out of the champagne bottle. In the background, she could hear the tinkling of wind chimes on a nearby grave.

She wouldn't even pay for the perpetual care for his grave. If his children wanted to, that was their business, but frankly, she'd done everything for Ryan she would ever do.

She poured herself a glass of champagne and sat on his headstone. Yes, it was disrespectful, according to her mother, but she didn't care. He was just lucky she didn't have the marker repossessed. If she had known then what she knew now, his funeral would have been budget all the way.

A cardboard box to bury the cheater in would have been good enough.

"I'd like to make a toast to you," she said. "To hiding your secrets well, may you rot in hell."

She lifted her glass and drained the alcohol. "This is good-bye, Ryan. I will never come back here. Tomorrow, we load up the U-Haul trailer and I'm returning to Texas. There the house is paid for, and hopefully, I will figure out what I'm going to do for the rest of my life. If you had not cashed in the life insurance policy, I would have that to live on. But now I'm going to have to find some kind of job."

All she could think about was going back to school and becoming a professor. She didn't want to teach in public school, but college might be the way to go. But for now, she had the summer to decide. And strangely enough, she was looking forward to being on the ocean.

Lifting the champagne bottle, she poured some of it on his grave. It was a three-hundred-dollar bottle of champagne, but she didn't care. They had saved it to drink at their silver wedding anniversary which they would never reach. And even if they had, their marriage had been a sham.

"Alex is doing much better now that we talked about what he saw that day with you and Lily. He graduated high school and the baseball team is in the playoffs. Taylor is in London. So many things you're missing out on in our children's lives. But then they were never important to you, only your practice and your mistress."

The wind blew her dark hair and she pushed the strands out of her face.

"You kept secrets from me, but I also have my secrets. When I was seventeen, I gave a baby up for adoption. Not my choice, but my mother's. She's contacted me, and as soon as I get settled, I'm going to respond to her letter. I planned on telling you about her the night you died."

She laughed as she thought of what Lily had told her.

"I must say, Ryan, you went out with one final orgasm, just

not with your wife. So embarrassing how you died. I'm sure the paramedics had a good laugh at your expense. And yes, Lily had to tell me to make me feel bad. But it didn't work. You see, by that time, I had already learned the truth about you."

She took another sip of the bubbly. "My plans had been to come here and rant and yell at you and ask how you could do this to me. But frankly, in the last month, I've come not to care about you. Whatever love I had died when I learned how you spent our money. How you had a great time making us broke. But don't worry, Lily's home has given me enough to live on for a year."

With a clench of her fists, she looked up at the sky. "Five years you kept that woman right under my nose. Alex and Kyle were best friends and now they barely speak. You were once a brilliant surgeon, and now, your life will only be remembered for the pain you caused. You are now called Dr. Plastic Dick."

She finished up her glass of champagne, knowing this was good-bye.

"You're going to love this. I'm pulling the trailer to Texas with the Porsche. Your beautiful sports car is going to be driven by me. I'm looking forward to cruising with it on the island. Hot widow woman with a beautiful sports car."

With a sigh, she stood and glanced down at the headstone.

"Good-bye Ryan. Thank you for my children. I'm going to do my best to remove your image and your name from my memory. Our life together was nothing but lies, only I didn't realize it until your death. Rest in Hell, Dr. Plastic Dick."

Walking back to the car, tears filled her eyes. This last month, it seemed all she did was cry, and today was the last time she would ever shed tears for Ryan again. It was over. He was dead and now she was going to begin her life over again.

Time to return to Mustang Island. Time to face her past.

CHAPTER 8

The next day, Alex and she packed up the rental trailer. The attorney had helped her straighten out her finances and even gotten her the money from the sale of Lily's house. Ryan had been stupid enough to put it in his name, not Lily's. The equity had doubled in five years and that money would help her start over.

Part of her felt bad she'd kicked the woman out, but then she thought of how she'd lived five years a couple doors away while Lily had an affair with her husband and felt no remorse.

Lily would now find some other man to sponge off. And she was certain it wouldn't take her long to find another rich man. After all, with her body built by Ryan, she could temp the richest with her big boobs, rounded hips, and narrow waist with a fresh facelift to remove the wrinkles.

"Mom, why do we have to move to Texas?"

"Because I have a house there that I own free and clear,"

she said. "Besides, you're going off to college this fall, your sister is in school and it will be just me."

"I don't like the idea of you being by yourself," Alex said.

In the last month, she'd seen her son return. Not the same bubbly kid, but a more refined version of himself.

But what she loved the most was how protective of her he had become.

After they spoke that night, Alex made a big effort to bring his grades up and had even written a letter to his college advisor telling him why his grades dipped. It was like the death of his father released him from the secret he'd been carrying. The secret he knew would hurt his mother.

She was so proud of him. Now she felt confident that he would become a strong, respectful man.

Together they made the decision not to tell Taylor about her father until she returned from England. Though Taylor also didn't understand why her mother was moving to Texas. But the idea of spending the summer on the beach had enticed her daughter enough that she would be coming to Texas at the end of the month.

Jennifer had booked the two kids' flights to arrive at the same time, and already, she was eager for them to meet her in Texas.

"I would be by myself if I stayed here," she said, thinking there was no way she was able to live here and glance down the street and see where her husband had housed his mistress for five years. Besides, the taxes and the cost of living in California were astronomical and she could no longer afford what it cost.

Damn Ryan.

Thank goodness, the house had sold quickly. When she called the mortgage company, they had told her she was behind by three months. She'd made enough money on both houses that she paid the mortgage loans in full, paid off the credit cards, and paid the employees at his office.

Everything was all nice and tidy and the lawyer had taken care of it all. Of course, his bill was outrageous, but she didn't care.

"Do you want me to stay and watch you play baseball," she asked Alex.

They had talked about it, but she had to be out of the house and she would have to stay in a hotel. She'd rather head to Texas and get out of Hollywood. Put the past behind her and prepare for her new life.

The paper had run an article on her husband and someone in his office admitted he was cheating on her and was behind in paying the employees. She didn't know who and didn't want to know.

The paper did not paint a nice picture of Ryan, but her only worry was keeping the article from Taylor. Thank goodness she was in London, or she feared she would have seen the searing account of her father.

"If I don't stay, I'll watch it on the internet. When you make your big play, I'll be in Texas screaming for you."

He grinned.

"No, I know you need to leave and put this place behind you."

She really did. For a week, she'd dodged reporters who wanted to know who her husband's mistress was and what did he do with all the money he made? If she replied, she knew it would not have been nice, so she avoided them.

She and her son carried the last boxes out of the house and put them in the trailer. She had sold most of the furniture and was mainly taking memorabilia. She preserved her wedding pictures and was going to make an album for each of her children. They could have them, she was done.

Some of the other pictures of Ryan, she planned on having a bonfire at the beach one night and having a weenie roast with another bottle of expensive champagne. A toast to new beginnings.

"Come on, let's go back through the house one more time," she said, wrapping her arm around her son's waist.

They opened the door into the kitchen and she remembered all the parties, the family get-togethers, everything that had happened in this room.

"I loved this kitchen," she told her son.

"I'm going to miss Esmeralda," he said.

She'd let the staff go almost immediately when she'd learned of their dire financial straits. No need to pay people to do work she could do.

"Me too," she said, knowing she would not have a housekeeper in Texas. It would only be her and she didn't need hired help.

They walked into the main family area with the big fireplace and the large windows overlooking the pool.

"It was a great place to grow up," Alex said.

Her parents had never lived this kind of life, and she couldn't imagine growing up in a house this large. She felt proud that her children had good memories. It was a shame their father ruined the image.

They walked through the rest of the house and in each room they commented on a special memory they had of the place. It was a sad final walk-through, but it was also closure. The end of this chapter of their lives.

Finally, with a sigh, they walked back down the stairs. It was time to go.

"Mom, please be safe," Alex said. "You'll call me every night and tell me where you are?"

"Of course," she said, realizing her son had become the protector. The worrier.

She was his only parent now, and she'd already had her will rewritten to make certain her children would be cared for if something happened to her. One thing Ryan's heart attack had done was shown her the finality of life could happen at any time.

"Come on, time to go," she said, climbing into the car. Alex's bags were in the back. He was staying with one of his friends until after the baseball season. Then he would fly to Texas with his sister.

As they drove away from the house for the last time, a sense of emptiness filled her. Who would have known that three months ago her life would change completely, that she would be starting over in the place she had run from?

Who knew what awaited her there?

CHAPTER 9

Jennifer took her time driving east to Texas, going slowly pulling the trailer, the top down on the Porsche as she watched the last of the California coast disappear. The first night, she stayed in San Diego since it was late afternoon when she pulled away from Alex's friend's house.

It had been hard to leave him behind, but she knew she would soon see him, and this gave her time to get the house ready for when the kids arrived. It had been twenty-six years since she'd seen her childhood summer home and had no idea what kind of shape it was in.

Hopefully all it needed was a little paint and maybe fresh carpet.

With the radio blasting, she turned down the street and pulled the Porsche into the drive. With a tired sigh, she climbed out of the car. The sound of ocean waves hitting the beach welcomed her and she took a deep breath of the sea air.

A sense of peace overcame her. She was home.

Going up to the door, she put the key in and went inside. Same eighties decor.

Dustcloths covered the furniture, and yet a layer of sand covered everything. After walking through the house, she opened the back door that led to the lower deck and the sight of the ocean greeted her. With a sigh, she watched the waves crashing on the shore.

Why had she waited so long to return?

Slowly she took the steps down to the beach, drawn by the ocean.

"Jennifer," she heard an older woman's voice call out to her, "is that you?"

Barbara White. The old grumpy woman herself.

She turned toward her. "Hello, Mrs. White."

"You're back?"

"Yes, I am," she said.

"Are you staying the summer?"

"No, I'm here for good," she said, grinning, a feeling of relief overwhelming her.

The older woman had to be nearing eighty, yet she all but ran down to meet her.

"You're moving in?"

"Yes, I am," she said.

"Divorced?"

"No, widowed," she told her, thinking a divorce would have been easier.

"Sorry to hear that," she said as she came up to her. "George has been gone for ten years. Your parents died before my George."

"Yes," Jennifer said, breathing in the wonderful fresh salt air. After crossing West Texas and the cattle processing plants, the smell of the ocean was a welcome relief.

The woman gazed over her. "Hell, you'll be remarried by summer. The single men around here are going to be flocking to your door."

Startled at her suggestion, Jennifer started laughing.

"Well, it's true," the older woman said.

If only she knew her past, she would understand Jennifer's hesitation. Oh hell no, she wasn't getting married again.

"My husband has only been in the ground for a little over a month. I'm not interested in men. Have no desire to get married again."

The woman frowned. "You're too young to be alone."

How many times had she heard this statement in the last month? It didn't matter. After what Ryan did, she didn't want to be involved with any man.

"No, I'm not," she said, thinking how weird it was that the older woman was so interested in her getting remarried. Was this what she had to look forward to?

"I've got to go. I have a trailer to unpack. I need to make a grocery store run and the house needs a thorough cleaning. I've got to get prepared for when my children arrive."

"You got kids?"

"Yes, a girl and a boy. They'll both be in college next year," she said, missing them. Taylor limited her calls to once a week, but Alex and she spoke daily.

She couldn't wait to call Alex tonight and tell him she was here. Taylor and she would talk on Sunday.

"If you need anything, you know where to find me," the old woman said. "Be aware that the cops are not allowing wild parties on the beach any longer."

The sun was beating down on Jennifer and she wanted to go in and get out of the heat for a few moments while she made a grocery list.

"Good to know. I haven't been to a wild party since college," she said.

"And we don't allow dope smoking here," she said. "I see you came from California and that cooky tobacco is legal there."

Where the hell was this coming from? It was all she could do to keep from cracking up with laughter from the woman's expression. Like Jennifer even knew what the laws were concerning marijuana. Drugs were something she'd never considered.

"Thanks for letting me know," she said. "Now I think I'll get out of the sun. Good to see you again, Mrs. White. I'm sure we'll chat again soon."

Of course, they would be chatting again; the woman was the biggest snoop.

Turning, she hurried back up the beach and into the house, laughing. She'd forgotten all about the old lady until now. It was certainly going to be a different life here. The homes were beach homes, not Beverly Hills mansions.

Simple beach cottages that she loved.

A new beginning.

Going through the house, room by room, it had been left exactly as she remembered it. The same eighties-style furniture covered by dust covers. The same macrame hangers, the old curtains, the old shells from time spent on the beach. The place needed a makeover, but first it needed a thorough cleaning. Today, she would tackle the kitchen, bathroom, and master bedroom.

For the next three hours, she threw out dust covers, vacuumed, turned on the water heater, and thoroughly scrubbed the three rooms she needed. The others would come later.

As darkness fell, she unhooked the trailer, found the few groceries she'd brought with her, and made the decision to go on a food run.

She jumped into the Porsche and went to the grocery store. As she walked the aisles, she realized she was no longer in California. Even the grocery store was more limited and did not have shelves of caviar and expensive wines.

As she rounded the wine aisle, she heard a voice.

"Jennifer? Is that you?"

Whirling around, she came face to face with her childhood friend Amanda Clark. She hadn't seen her since the summer of 1996.

"Amanda," she cried and they rushed into one another's arms.

Sure, they had exchanged Christmas cards, but they had not seen each other since that time.

"What are you doing here?"

"I've moved back," she said not wanting to delve into all the reasons why. It was her first day back and she was determined to leave Dr. Plastic Dick back in California.

"You still live here?"

"Oh yes," she said.

"This calls for a celebration. What is your phone number?" she asked.

They exchanged numbers and Amanda squealed and jumped up and down. This called for a get-together.

"I see the others occasionally, but this deserves a night out on the town," she said.

"Give me at least a week. My children arrive in a month and I've got to get the house ready for them. I just arrived this afternoon and came by to pick up a few groceries."

"No problem, that will give me time to pull this together," she said. "It's been so long."

"Twenty-six years since I've been here," she said. "I didn't even come when Mom and Dad died."

She had planned on never returning to the island after what she suffered here. But here she was, and now it felt right for some odd reason.

"Have you heard about Paige?"

Paige McClane was one of their wildest friends. Known for her outlandish partying ways, they had lost touch after Jennifer went to college.

"No," she said, wondering what the girl had done.

"She's a big hot-shot executive up in Boulder, Colorado," Amanda said softly. She leaned forward. "She's still her wild self."

Jennifer smiled. "Good for her."

She had believed her life was all good and wonderful, only to learn her husband had been cheating on her.

Maybe she should have lived a wild life. Maybe at least she would have found a man who adored her.

"Maybe when she learns you're here, she'll come down for a visit," Amanda said.

"It would be great to see her," Jennifer said.

She glanced down at her basket, knowing she needed to finish and get back to the house.

"I'll let you go, but if you need anything call me," Amanda said.

"I do need one thing," she said. "The furniture has not been replaced for probably thirty years. Where is the best place to buy furniture?"

"Corpus Christi," Amanda replied. "Here on the island, we're still pretty remote."

"Thanks," she said, thinking she wanted to replace it all, but she would have to take a good hard look at her funds.

"Good night," Amanda said, turning her grocery basket and heading toward the door.

Jennifer finished her shopping, and after she got back to the house, she unpacked a few boxes that held her personal items, setting them up in the master bedroom. Then she ate the supper she had picked up at the grocery store out on the deck.

As she watched the sun go down, she listened to the waves and sipped from her wine glass. Why did it feel like she'd come home?

Why did this feel like this was where she belonged?

Going inside, she pulled the letter from Madison out of her purse and reread it.

Maybe this was a time of healing for all those she loved. And she did love this daughter she hadn't seen in twenty-five years. Maybe it was time to answer her letter and let the recovery begin.

CHAPTER 10

Breakfast was a simple bagel with cream cheese. Last night, she'd unpacked her coffee pot, and this morning she had breakfast out on the deck, watching the people walk the beach, enjoying the breeze and the sound of the surf.

It was time to write Madison. The young woman probably thought she didn't want to speak to her, but she was so wrong. Life had dealt Jennifer a blow that had been hard to recover from. But now was the time for her to contact her daughter. She'd waited so very long to speak to her.

With a sigh, she picked up the pen. This morning, her mind was fresh and clear and she wanted to get this done before she changed her mind.

Shaking, she picked up a pen and began to write.

Dearest Madison,

Yes, I'm your mother. Not a day has gone by that I haven't thought about you. Not a day has gone by that I haven't prayed for your safety and that you were receiving the love you deserved.

I'm glad you reached out to me. I've thought about contacting you several times, but I didn't want to upset your life. Forgive me that it took so long for me to respond, but the day I received your letter, my husband died of a heart attack. Since then I've been dealing with the will and all the things that must be done when a person dies.

After his death, I made the decision to return to Texas and I'm now living on Mustang Island. I would tell you to come tomorrow, but I'm trying to get the house prepared for when my other children arrive.

They do not know about you and I would love you to visit, just the two of us before they get here. It would give me a chance to explain my reasons for letting you go. It would also give us time to get to know one another. How about if you come in two weeks? The house has four bedrooms, so there is plenty of room for you to stay.

Here is my phone number. Call me and let me know if you can come then.

Love,

Jennifer

Oh dear God, she hoped this was the right thing to do. Before she could change her mind, she sealed the letter in an envelope and filled out the address. The only problem was her stamps were still inside the trailer in a box labeled office supplies. Who knew when she would get to them?

But the post office was just a block away. She needed to see if she had any forwarded mail and see about getting a box. They had laughed at her when she called and told them she was moving into the house.

No one had ever lived here permanently until now.

Putting on her hat and shades, she picked up the envelope and her purse and then walked out the door. The sun was already beating down, and she knew this afternoon she would have to close the windows and let the air conditioner run. The afternoons were hot and the evenings were a delight with the ocean breeze blowing in.

Last night had been such a joy to sleep to the sounds of the ocean, the crashing of the waves, and the breeze blowing through the open window.

The old house creaked and groaned at night, but she had not been afraid. It desperately needed to be remodeled. And she wondered if she could do it all before her kids arrived.

A lady waved to her as she walked along the sand-covered street and she returned the wave. No one in Hollywood waved at each other unless it was a star. Then it was expected. But the island was small, and she knew that sooner or later, she would probably know most of these people.

Many of them would remember her from the summers she stayed here with her parents.

As she rounded the corner, there was the post office, a small wooden building. She wondered how many hurricanes it had withstood. The island had not had a direct hit from a hurricane in over fifty years.

Stepping up to the door, she gripped the handle and

backed out of the way as a handsome man came charging out.

"Excuse me," he said and then he stopped, his mouth dropped open and he stared at her. "Jennifer?"

Shit, oh shit, oh shit. She couldn't be here twenty-four hours without running into Dylan. Not even a full day and here he was and the letter…shit!

"Dylan," she said coldly, knowing she did not want to get involved with any man and especially not this one.

It was all she could do to be civil to him when she wanted to rail at him about not contacting her. How he had broken her teenage heart.

"Are you back for the summer? This is the first time in over twenty-five years I've seen you on the island."

How did she respond? There were so many questions, and yet she wanted nothing to do with him.

"I just returned and I'll be here permanently. Are you here for the summer?"

"No, I'm also a permanent resident," he said as he stepped out of the way for someone else to leave the building.

Damn, he still looked like he did twenty-six years ago, but now there were streaks of gray in his hair which made him look very distinguished. Very handsome. His dark brown eyes twinkled with excitement.

He shook his head at her. "Maybe we can have coffee sometime. Catch up."

Oh hell no. This was why she had not returned for a quarter century. There would be no catching up with

Dylan. No finding out that he knew about the pregnancy and deliberately avoided her.

"Sure," she said lying, wanting him to walk away. "I'm really busy right now. I'm redoing the old house."

Reaching into his pocket, he pulled out a card with his name and phone number on it, that she knew she would promptly throw away.

"Thanks," she said.

"What's your number," he asked.

Crap! How did she get out of this? A smile crossed her face as she gave him Dr. Plastic Dick's cell number. She'd turned it off and gave the phone away. It was not a working number. But Dylan didn't know that, and frankly, she didn't care.

"Thanks! I'd really like to hear why you just disappeared."

What was he talking about? She'd written him letters and he never responded.

"I'd like to know why you never answered my letters," she said, unable to keep her tone even as much as she'd like to.

How dare he accuse her of disappearing when he never responded to her calls or her letters.

Pinched lines appeared between his eyes as his brows pulled together. "Look I've got to go. I have an appointment in five minutes, but we need to catch up."

"Sure," she said, knowing it would never happen.

"You look great," he said.

"Thank you," she replied as she wondered if he was married. But it didn't matter because she didn't care. There were so many secrets between them, it would not be wise to see him again.

"Soon, we'll catch up," he said before he turned and walked away. The sway of his manly body was still as tempting as it was back then. But that was then, and today, she was a different person.

"Son of a bitch," she said softly. "Can't be in town for twenty-four hours before I run into Dylan."

Opening the door, she hurried into the post office eager to do her business and then get back to the house. Holding up the letter in her hand, she almost didn't mail it because everything would soon be revealed.

Taking a deep breath, she bought a book of stamps and then shoved it into the outbox. What had she just done?

CHAPTER 11

By the time she returned to the house, the heat had drained her, and yet she had so many things to do. She fixed a big pitcher of sweet ice tea and rested on the deck, watching people play in the surf. She was back in Texas and nothing was better in the summer than a glass of sweet tea.

Nothing was better than watching people on the beach.

Her phone rang and she glanced down at the number. She didn't recognize it, so she ignored the call.

After she rested, she took her notepad and pen, and went from room to room taking note of what needed to be done. All three bathrooms needed to be remodeled. There was painting to do, and she was going to take down those god-awful ugly curtains that had been there since her childhood.

It was a wonder they were not in tatters as old as they were.

In the garage, she found a ladder and decided to remove

all the drapes. They had to go and then she was going to order blinds for all the rooms.

The trailer had to be unloaded today and she cleared an upstairs room to hold the extra boxes until she knew what she wanted to do with them. But she wasn't unloading that trailer until the temperatures went down. She'd forgotten how hot it could be in Texas.

As she glanced around the room, nothing seemed to have been removed since her parents last visit here. They had not been to the house several years prior to their deaths. The drive down from Dallas was long and her mother and father got to where they couldn't drive long distances.

Sadly, she didn't visit them much. It wasn't fair to keep the grandkids away from them, so twice a year they flew to Texas. Of course, Dr. Plastic Dick was always too busy to go with them. His patients needed him.

Probably more like his latest mistress.

Now she realized he put everything before his family. There were so many things she was no longer willing to accept. It would take a courageous man to date her and have a relationship with her. But that would only happen way in the future. Right now, she had a house to remodel.

Pushing the thoughts aside, she went inside and began to work on the living room. She went through all the end tables, the cabinets, even the pictures, and decided which ones she wanted to keep. This was the room she would start in. Then she made a list of what furnishings she needed.

All of this furniture could be classified as antique. Not good ones, but just really old.

After that, she removed the sad, old paintings on the walls that showed how much the paint had faded. These pictures were relics from the eighties. She made two stacks; one was donations and one trash.

The doorbell rang and she frowned. Who knew she was here? Who would come calling now? Glancing through the window, she saw a man with a bouquet of flowers in his hand. This had better not be from Dylan or they would be shoved back in the man's face.

Opening the door, she frowned and signed for the bouquet. "Before you leave, I need to see who they are from."

She ripped open the envelope and her heart filled with love.

Welcome back! We're so glad you're here. Let's have dinner soon. Amanda, Nicole, Paige, and Crystal.

Even Paige knew she had returned. But would she be at the dinner they were planning?

Immediately she understood who was calling her, her old friends. Girls from high school she had grown up with. Their summers had been spent splashing and swimming in the ocean every day. Carefree days before life grabbed them by the throat and showed them what was to come.

"Thank you," she said, taking the bouquet and closing the door.

These weren't funeral flowers, but *welcome back, we love you* flowers and she was thrilled. She set them on the dining room table and smiled. This made her so happy that her friends had remembered her.

They wanted to go to dinner but was she ready to tell them what happened to her? There would be questions about why she had never returned. Why hadn't she returned their calls?

What happened to her?

It was like she'd stepped off the earth twenty-six years ago and only reappeared this year. How could she invite them over to a house that looked like it was still in the eighties?

Maybe she should put on some disco music. A giggle erupted from her at the thought. The theme song could be *Stayin' Alive*.

Glancing around the house, she knew that her funds were not the best, but if she were going to live here, she had no choice but to upgrade this house. Otherwise, she would be living in the past and she needed the future.

"Damn, Mom, don't you think you could have at least updated the curtains?" she said out loud.

It was almost overwhelming how much work the house needed.

The doorbell rang again, and this time, she answered it without checking to see who was there.

When she yanked open the door, Dylan stood in front of her.

Shit! She knew better than to just open the door. But she'd expected Amanda or one of her other friends.

"We've got to talk," he said, walking past her and into

the house. "You said something this morning that has bothered me all day."

This was not what she needed. The sooner he left the better.

"As you can see, I'm a little busy," she said, thinking there was so much work to do. "If you barge in, you have to work."

He ignored her. "You said I never answered your letters. What letters? I never received anything from you. Nothing. It was like you disappeared into thin air."

She didn't want to do this now. And what he was telling her didn't fit with her side of the story at all. How many letters had she written him that he never answered?

Suddenly it was like he saw the inside of the house for the first time. "Boy, this is like stepping back in time."

"Yes," she said. "I haven't unpacked the trailer yet and I have to return it tomorrow."

He leaned against the Formica counter tops in the kitchen. He'd aged well and was still as handsome as he'd been at seventeen. Even now, her body felt attracted to him.

No. Just no. No more men. Stick a fork in her, she was done with marriage, men, and relationships.

"I tell you what, I will help you unload the trailer if you'll agree to have dinner with me tomorrow night."

Really? Did he think they would talk and everything would be worked out? That they could start up right where they left off? There was no way she was going to get involved with him again.

She glanced at him and shook her head. "No. I can unload it myself."

"Oh come on, Jennifer, it's just for old time's sake and to catch up. Something happened that summer that separated us and I don't know what. I'd like to learn why I never heard from you. You broke my teenage heart."

What about her own teenage heart? He bruised it pretty badly himself.

Yes, she did know what happened. And she wasn't going to tell him about her daughter. As for his teenage heart she had no sympathy. All he had to do was answer her letters.

What if it hadn't been on purpose? What if somehow her mother had managed to interfere again?

"I'll even give you the name of a good paint and tile guy," he said. "I think you're going to need him."

That was worth its weight in gold. For that, she would have dinner with him, one time, one night, and never again.

"All right, I'll go to dinner with you not tomorrow night but Saturday night."

"Can't do that," he said. "My children are coming to visit Friday night through Monday. I could do Tuesday."

Oh, this was good. She could drag this out. "How about next Thursday night?"

"I don't like waiting that long. I need some answers," he told her. "Why not tell me now. We're alone, you could answer all my questions."

Did he really think she cared? She'd been just as hurt by

his non-response. In fact, she kind of liked making him wait. Dragging out the torture just a little longer.

"You'll have to wait," she said. "Now are you going to help me unload the trailer?"

She really could use his help. Alex was in California, and he'd done most of the work. She'd forgotten how heavy some of those boxes were.

A frown spread across his face, his big brown eyes narrowed, and she could see he was frustrated. Too bad. Right now, men were not at the top of her list of people she wanted to make happy.

And he was right below Dr. Plastic Dick.

Picking up her keys, she strolled out the door. The sun was still beaming its scorching-hot rays. The latch was hot to the touch as she unlocked the trailer.

"There you go," she said. "As you carry them in, I'll tell you where they go."

"You're not going to help?"

A grin spread across her face. "Of course, I am. I'm going to tell you where to put each box. There's only about one hundred."

Shaking his head, he gave a little laugh. "I really stepped into shit, didn't I."

"You got what you wanted. Dinner with me next Thursday."

"If I'm not dead," he said.

"Yes, please don't have a heart attack. A dead husband and an ex-boyfriend in two months dying from the same thing might appear a little suspicious."

His brows drew together and he frowned. "I'm sorry to hear that."

"Don't be. After he died, I learned he was cheating on me. Dr. Plastic Dick is no more."

Laughter spewed from him and he grinned at her. "This is what I remember about you. Your smart-ass attitude. It was what drew me to you."

That was not what she needed to hear. Maybe instead of having a smart-ass attitude, she should just go for bitch.

"Well, don't get too close. My armor is up, my shield is protecting me, and currently, men are not my favorite people."

"Good. Women are not mine either."

Laughter came from her and she leaned back. "We might could be friends after all."

"That is if you don't kill me unloading this trailer."

"One less man on the planet can't be a bad thing," she said. "I'll be waiting in the house for you to carry in the boxes."

With that, she turned and went inside. He'd made this deal and he could live with it.

An hour later, when everything was unloaded, she handed him a tall glass of tea.

Sweat ran down his face and he breathed hard, but she'd not had to unload the trailer.

"If I had my bathing suit on, we could go for a swim in the ocean."

The memory of them swimming and playing in the waves rocked her for a moment. They had been so naive and young. So fearless and so in love. Nothing was going to stop them and yet...

"I haven't stopped long enough to enjoy the ocean. My kids are coming in a month, and I want to have a lot of this work done on the house."

He nodded. "Understand. I'll text you the tile and paint guy."

Oh crap! She had given him Dr. Plastic Dick's phone number.

"You know, you mentioned two daughters, but you haven't said if you're married or not. I can't have a married man in my home."

Yes, it was a little late to ask, but after what Ryan did, she would not be part of destroying a marriage. She would not become a Lily.

A smile formed on his handsome face that was beet red from the exertion and the sun. "Relax. I'm divorced. I have two girls. I'm a wonderful father and a great ex-husband."

Good. She could let him stay. But her guard would remain up.

"There's something I need to tell you. This morning when I ran into you at the post office, I gave you Dr. Plastic Dick's phone number."

"What? Who are you talking about?"

She giggled. "That's what I call my dead husband. Maybe someday I'll explain why, but not now. Here's my real phone number. Don't call me."

A grin spread across his face.

"Don't worry. You don't like men and I've been betrayed by way too many women to want another one."

Her brows raised. "Is that so? I guess you include me in there?"

"As a matter of fact, I do. Now, if you'll excuse me, I need to go home, take a shower, shoot some nude photos and send you some dick pics."

This was a part of life she had no experience in and wanted no part of lewd photos.

"Go ahead. I promise to show them to the girls I'm having dinner with and my son in a month. He's a pretty husky guy, and he's very protective of his mother."

The Dylan she knew would never do something so promiscuous, but it had been twenty-six years. Maybe he'd changed and that was why women no longer wanted him.

"If I send them to you will you send me pictures of you?"

She knew he was teasing her. He always teased and cut up, but she liked to give it right back to him.

"Sure, I'll send you some pictures. How about one with my dead husband lying in the casket. How would you like that? Or I could send you a picture of his mistress. She's a real piece of work. Which would you prefer?"

Shaking his head, he sighed. "Still a pain in the ass, aren't you?"

"Oh, I became tame and life kicked me in the butt. So I'm going to stir up and cause as much shit as possible. No more being a dutiful wife and mother. I think I want to be a hellraiser and see if Barbara will report me to the HOA."

He laughed, his eyes twinkling in that way she remembered. "One problem, we don't have an HOA."

"Then, maybe, I should start one," she said, putting a finger on her chin.

"I don't have time for this bullshit," he said. "I'm going home and taking a shower, cooking dinner, and getting the guest rooms ready for my girls. You mentioned a boy, do you just have the one child?"

"No, I have three," she said, thinking she was no longer going to avoid saying that she had only two children. Time for the hurting to heal. Time for her to accept the child she'd given up.

"Get out of here," she said. "Unless you want to help me unbox things and put them away. Then you can stay."

"Oh hell no," he said and turned to the door. "You've already roped me into unloading the trailer. I think I'm done for the evening."

He walked out the door and then turned back. "Good evening, Jennifer. I'm glad you're back. Sooner or later, you're going to tell me the truth. Sooner or later, we're going to have that conversation."

"Agreed," she replied. "And sooner or later, you're going to tell me why you didn't answer my letters."

Shaking his head, he walked down the street and she closed the door behind him. Was she playing with fire? Maybe, but she'd been burned long enough by not playing with fire, and right now, she felt like she was invincible. No one could hurt her any longer.

Bring her the matches because she was ready to burn some shit down.

CHAPTER 12

Jennifer looked through the closet trying to find something smart and hip to wear. Something that didn't scream old lady or mother. And she refused to wear black. Maybe it was wrong, but the way she planned to honor Ryan's death was by beginning again.

Starting over.

Today, she'd taken the trailer into Corpus Christi and turned it in. The man had laughed at her when she drove up in the Porsche.

"That's something I never thought I'd see," he said. "A Porsche pulling a trailer."

"Got the job done," she said. "Besides I wanted my dead husband to look down and see how I used his sports car."

The man glanced at her like she was crazy, but she didn't care. Right now, she felt a little on the wackadoodle side.

After that, she went shopping for new furniture and

picked out some pieces she thought fit the house very well. She had spoken to the paint and tile guy that Dylan recommended. He would start work on the bathrooms and the kitchen next week.

To save money, she was going to be painting the walls herself. It had been many years since she'd painted, but sometimes you did what you had to do. And this would save her at least eight thousand dollars. Money that could buy new blinds.

Plus, she had such a hankering to put in a new folding glass door across the back, but first, she wanted to ask if they were good during a hurricane. But the idea of the glass doors being thrown open to let the ocean breeze in thrilled her.

Though she was putting in new white wooden blinds in the bedrooms, she'd bought gauzy curtains to go over the living room windows, and she'd found a soft teal color that matched the ocean to paint the walls.

How she was going to get all of this done before the kids arrived, she didn't know, but she wanted them to love it here. No, it was not their house in Beverly Hills, but she hoped it would be even better.

Their family would soon no longer have any secrets. And she wanted this house to feel like their home. A place where they spent their summers.

Tomorrow she planned on beginning the painting. The furniture would be delivered next week, and Monday, the tile crew would arrive. He said he could get both bathrooms and the kitchen completed in two weeks. She hoped so.

Pulling out a summer dress, she slipped it over her head, put on sandals, grabbed her purse, and walked down the beach to the restaurant. One thing she loved about living here was being able to walk to most places. Sure it had grown from when she was seventeen, but still she liked keeping the Porsche parked in the garage out of the sun, sand, and salty air.

It took her ten minutes to stroll down the beach, and the first person she saw was Amanda running to her.

"Hi," she said, grabbing her. "You look gorgeous."

"Thanks," she said. "Not bad for a forty-something mother."

Amanda laughed. "The others are inside. Come on, this is going to be so much fun."

When they walked in, she saw the others sitting at a table with a view of the ocean.

The waves rolled in calmly and crested when they reached the shore.

They all screamed and she hugged each woman realizing how much she'd missed them, and wondering if their lives had been anything like hers. Hoping they were each happy.

Nicole hugged her tight. "It's so good to see you."

"You too," Jennifer said, knowing it was true.

Crystal, the blonde bombshell, bumped her with her hip like she did when they were kids. "Damn, girl, I think you got better looking with age. I'm so glad you're back. Don't just drop out of sight again."

"Me too," she said, bumping her hips back. "And you're

still the same stinking beauty that the men can't get enough of. Don't worry, I'm not leaving again."

"Oh hell, if you only knew, honey. I think I hate men."

"Me too," Jennifer said with a laugh. "Even dead ones."

They all looked at her strangely as they took their seats at the table.

"Thank you for the flowers today. They were so thoughtful and made me feel very special."

"Good," Amanda said. "We're so happy you're back."

For the next ten minutes, they looked at the menu and ordered either wine or a cocktail of their choice.

"Who is married?" Jennifer asked, not ready to tell them about why she'd returned.

"I am," Amanda said. "And I have five children. The last one goes off to college this year. Then we'll be free to go see the world."

"Nicole, are you married?"

"No, I'm a lawyer," she said. "I work to put criminals behind bars."

"We've been trying to hook her up with men for years, but she's very picky," Amanda said.

"Good for you," Jennifer said.

"Not everyone can have a great husband like you have, Amanda."

"Oh, Eric is a good father and husband," she said. "We've been married for nearly twenty-six years."

"What about you, Crystal?"

The blonde smiled and shook her head. "I keep searching for the right man with no luck. I've been dating a man and I think he's getting close to asking me to marry him. But I don't know. Maybe I'm not meant to be married."

"Paige is not meant to be married," Amanda said and then leaned forward. "Aaron is going to propose?"

Crystal smiled. "I think so. We've been talking about what we expect in a partner when we marry. He's a really nice guy. I'm just not sure."

Jennifer wanted to warn her to not do it, but she refrained. It wasn't her place to convince her friends they were making a huge mistake.

"Have you guys had sex?" Nicole asked. "You were complaining last time that he didn't seem to enjoy sex because you hadn't had it yet."

"Yes, we did have sex," she said blushing.

"And…" Amanda said.

She laughed. "You know I have yet to find a man who knows where the clitoris is."

Jennifer had just taken a sip of wine and she spewed it. "I agree with you."

Dr. Plastic Dick had never been particularly wonderful in the bedroom, and she'd often wondered if it was her. Maybe that's why he got Lustful Lily. Maybe she twisted and contorted that curvaceous body of hers around him and he found it meaningful.

"You're considering marrying this man and the sex is not good?"

Crystal sighed. "Look, I'm running out of time. My biological clock is a ticking time bomb and I want a family. He's a good man. He loves me. He takes good care of me; he's just not great in the bedroom."

The women snickered.

"Maybe you should buy him an instruction manual," Amanda said.

"Or introduce toys into your lovemaking," Nicole said.

"Or walk away and find someone who knows where your clitoris is and how to turn you on," Jennifer said and then shook her head. "Sorry, don't ask me for marital or men advice. I obviously am not good at it."

Just then the waitress delivered their orders and her mouth immediately began to water. Fresh shrimp from the gulf. Nothing was better.

"Another glass of wine, please." She told the girls two drinks were her limits, but damn, she deserved to have a good time tonight. This would be her third drink, and Dr. Plastic Dick always told her that was her danger zone. Where her mouth went into overdrive and she became the life of the party.

Tonight was a celebration. She was back with her old friends and she was redoing the beach house. Maybe she deserved to be the life of the party.

After they began to eat, Crystal glanced at her. "What happened to you?"

"Which time?" she asked with a giggle. "The first time I left the island or my reason for returning?" She shook her head. "Only one sad story per night. Tonight we'll start with my return."

The alcohol had affected her and she started to giggle. How would these women react to what she was about to tell them? The wine flowed through her body, but she didn't care, she was going to tell it all.

"My husband had a heart attack and died," she said laughing.

They all stopped eating and stared at her in shock. She could see they didn't know how to act because she was laughing about his death.

"I'm so sorry," Amanda said.

"Oh no, don't be sorry," she said, popping a piece of shrimp into her mouth. "He died with his penis inside his mistress."

There was a gasp around the table.

"Oh, it gets better. Dr. Plastic Dick bought his Lustful Lily a home two houses down from ours. Our son and her son played together and grew up together. Busy playing soccer mom, I had no idea my husband was cheating on me until after his death. Then his staff asked me to please pay them because he hadn't."

She took another bite of shrimp as the women all sat there staring at her.

"Two days after his funeral, where I was the grieving widow, I went to his office. There I learned the state of our affairs. He had not paid the taxes on his employees' income, he had not paid them in a month, he was behind on the rent of his office, on our mortgage, on Lily's mortgage, his car, the credit cards were maxed, and we were broke."

She gave a little laugh. "This man made over five million a year and he had squandered it all on a woman who lived down the street from us."

Laughing, she gazed at them. "But let me tell you, Lustful Lily looks like a million dollars. New boob job, facelift, tummy tuck, and a firm booty. She's been nipped and tucked and I wouldn't be surprised if her vagina had not been tightened."

They gasped

"They can do that?" Amanda asked.

"Oh yes," Jennifer said with a giggle. "If you have the money, they can tighten it up and make it almost virginal again."

With a deep breath, she went on to tell them how the lawyer she contacted took care of and got everything straightened out.

"And that is why I returned to Mustang Island. The house here is in my name and is paid for. I made enough from the sale of our house and Lustful Lily's house that I have enough to live on if I'm careful. I'm thinking of going back to school and becoming a professor."

"Dr. Plastic Dick and Lustful Lily…" Nicole said laughing. "You always could come up with the most bizarre names."

"That's better than dickhead," she said. "Or bitch."

"What kind of doctor was he," Crystal asked.

"He was known as the Plastic Surgeon to the Stars. He operated on some of the biggest names in Hollywood. Face lifts, nose reconstruction, eyebrow lifts, tummy tucks…you name it, he could do it."

"Did he ever work on you?" Amanda asked. "I mean you would have had free care."

"No, I didn't want facial surgery," Jennifer said, thinking of the fights they had because she refused to go under his knife. Now she wondered if she would have died on the operating table.

"That might have been a good thing," Nicole said.

"Exactly," Jennifer said. "He did work on our daughter and she's beautiful. But I didn't think it was necessary."

Amanda took a bite of her food and shook her head. "Well, damn, girl. You've lived quite the life."

"How did you find out he died with his penis in Lustful Lily?"

"She told me. After I learned where a lot of the money had gone, I went down to see her and we had a little discussion. She was the one who told me how he died."

"Bitch," Crystal said. "She could have kept that to herself."

For the first time in days, Jennifer felt tears well in her eyes. She didn't want to start crying in front of her friends. She'd believed that she was over the hurt of his deception. Obviously not.

Quickly she wiped them away.

"If you start crying, we'll all start crying," Amanda said. "Dr. Plastic Dick doesn't deserve your tears."

Jennifer started to laugh. She'd forgotten how these girls could help her feel better about anything. Oh, how she'd missed being with this group of ladies.

"You're right," she said. "And those tears were the first ones in two weeks. I took one of the bottles of champagne we'd been saving for our twenty-fifth wedding anniversary and I had it out at his grave. Told him this would be the last time he would see me. I hope the damn prairie dogs dig holes in his grave."

Nicole laughed. "You don't know how many times I hear this kind of stuff in the courtroom. And everyone wonders why I never married."

The rest of the evening, they laughed and joked and Jennifer felt happier than she had in months. It was so good to be back. So good to have returned to the island. So good to be with the friends who loved her.

"Wait a minute," Amanda said. "You said which time? You just disappeared from the island and never returned. What else happened to you?"

She wasn't ready to share that story. She wasn't ready to tell anyone, because she had yet to meet her daughter and she didn't want Dylan to learn he had three children.

"That, ladies, is a story for another day," she said.

"I'm hoping to have the house ready for company in two weeks. I have a ton of photos that I plan on burning in a bonfire on the beach. Anyone want to come and drink champagne and celebrate the end of my marriage?"

Crystal smiled. "I do, but damn, girl, you are taking this so much better than I would. And you have two children by this man. How are they taking this news?"

A sigh escaped from her. "Alex lived the situation and knows everything. Taylor has been away at college. She came home for the funeral, but at the time, I didn't know what Ryan had done. I've got to tell her. Right now, she's in England on a study trip, but she'll be here in a month and I have to tell her the truth about her father."

"Shit," Amanda said. "That's not going to be fun."

"No," Nicole said. "I don't envy you."

"Maybe I don't want children," Crystal said. "It sounds so complicated."

"I love my children with all my heart," Jennifer said. "Their dad was a shit, but he gave me wonderful children. And I even thanked him that day out at the cemetery. They are the best of him and I wouldn't trade them for anything."

What her friends didn't know was that there was so much more she was going to have to share with her children. So much of their lives seemed to have secrets and she was going to expose them all.

It was the only way to heal. It was the only way to fix the past. Time for the secrets to be revealed.

CHAPTER 13

The next morning, Jennifer woke with a wine hangover.

She couldn't remember the last time she'd had too much to drink and knew she didn't want to make a habit of consuming so much alcohol. It made her feel yucky.

"That was so stupid," she said to herself rising from bed. "You don't have time for this. You've got things to do today."

On a last-minute whim, she had decided to put down new flooring in the beach house. The carpet in the main room was shag – dirty shag left over from the seventies. There was no telling how much sand and dirt was in that old carpet.

The rest of the floors were vinyl and she wanted either tile or laminate flooring throughout the house. So another major project.

Getting up, she made her coffee, took a pain reliever, and sat outside on the deck in her house coat, having her breakfast. It was peaceful, quiet, and she loved watching the children play on the beach, their excited voices carrying as they squealed with laughter.

Why had it taken her this long to get back here? Dylan...she hadn't wanted to face him. It was easier to stay away and hate him than to see his handsome face once again.

Finally, feeling better, she walked back inside. Surveying the area, she decided to move the old furniture out to the curb. It was time to say good-bye. She kept very few sentimental pieces. Her grandfather's old clock, some photos of her parents, and a couple of knickknacks she remembered had been here since she'd been a child.

The rest she piled out on the trash pile.

If anyone was interested in old-fashioned furniture, it was there for the hauling.

Putting on a disposable mask, she began the task of ripping up the carpet and rolling it up. The tile man could take care of the bundle for her tomorrow. Then she cleaned the concrete slab beneath the old carpet from the many years of dirt and stains.

At lunch, she went back out on the deck, ate a sandwich, and rested.

It was odd, but she was enjoying the physical labor of redoing the beach house. It felt like she was cleaning out the garbage in her life and restoring the structure. Building the house from the floor up just like she was being rehabbed into a new woman.

A woman who would not accept a man's cheating or someone who was too busy with things other than his family. But for now, she didn't need anyone. Every day she felt stronger. Every day she realized she'd made the right decision moving here.

The rest of the afternoon she spent with a paint roller, slapping paint on the walls. When she finished the living room, she was stunned. The lighter color made the room feel bigger. Now she could see how the new furniture would look brightening up the room.

At four o'clock, she finished and sat to watch the baseball game her son was playing in. They were in the semifinals and she was so excited for him.

She texted him that she was sitting on the deck listening to the surf, watching him play.

For the next three hours, she watched as his team beat the other California high school team to advance to the next round. Alex played second base, and twice he tagged out a runner trying to steal.

The team had gathered on the field for their winning chant, when she saw out of the corner of her eye, Kyle running across the field, his face contorted with rage.

"Oh no," she cried unable to stop him so many miles away.

He came up behind Alex, whirled him around, and punched him in the face, knocking him to the ground. Alex jumped up ready to hit him back, but the coaches and the players intervened and stopped him.

Kyle was being held back by the players and coaches, screaming something at Alex. She could hear some words, but not all of them. *Your mother* was one phrase she heard screamed.

Alex said something back to him and Kyle struggled to get to him, but her son did the bravest thing. He shrugged out of the coaches' holds, turned, and walked away.

Love filled her heart and she wished she could hug Alex. Oh, how she missed her son. How she missed being with him every evening. How she missed their talks.

Proudly, he walked off the field and into the locker area.

Picking up her phone, she called him and he answered.

"I'm so proud of you," she said. "You played an excellent game and your team won."

"Yeah, it was a good game," he said.

"But more than anything, you did not engage with Kyle. You could have been kicked off the team for fighting him."

He laughed. "I know. Coach kept whispering in my ear *don't do it*. Mom, I do feel bad for Kyle, but his mother brought this on themselves."

"Well, your father played a huge role in it as well," she said not willing to place all the blame on Lustful Lily, though looking back she blamed herself. She should have paid more attention to Dr. Plastic Dick's schedule. She should have demanded he spend time with them as a family.

"You handled the situation like a grown man," she said sniffling.

"Are you crying?"

"Yes, you're my son and you're growing into a fine upstanding man. When you get here, I'm going to have to beat off the girls."

He laughed.

"When is your next game?"

"We travel to San Francisco tomorrow and play the next day," he said. "We have two more games before the championship."

How could she miss seeing him play? How could she miss his game if he made it all the way to the championship?

Money was tight, especially with the way she was spending so much on the old house trying to make it into a home for the kids and herself.

"If you make it to the championship, I'll fly out," she said, knowing the airfare was not what she needed to be spending money on right now. But her son deserved a parent there. Her son who had pulled himself out of the funk that overtook him when he learned his father was cheating.

"Let's wait and see," he said. "This next team has won state two years in a row."

"Just do your best," she said. "I'm so happy for you."

"Thanks, Mom," he said. "How's the house coming along?"

She sighed. "Today, I pulled up the old carpet in the living room, painted the walls, and tomorrow the tile man is coming. This place needs a lot of work."

"Mom, it's our new home; it's going to be okay," he said.

Damn, she loved this kid. Always making her feel like it would be all right as long as they were together, even if they had to live in a shack.

"I've got to go," he said. "Zachary's parents are here to pick us up."

"Love you," she said.

"You too," he replied and she realized he had a room full of teenage boys around him. What young man wanted to tell his mother he loved her in front of a group of boys?

Hanging up, it was all she could do not to call Lustful Lily and tell her if her boy touched Alex, he'd be in jail. Soon, miles would separate them and she could hardly wait. She was so ready to close that chapter of her life.

And yet, Alex felt sorry for Kyle.

Glancing around the room, she decided she'd worked hard enough for the day. Time to walk the beach and have some fun. She would put on her bathing suit and test out the ocean.

CHAPTER 14

*L*aughing, she dove into a cresting wave, swimming as far out as she felt safe, before she turned and headed back to shore. The water was cool, not hot, not warm and she had forgotten how much she enjoyed the ocean.

A school of fish darted in different directions in front of her. Water rippled around her as she bobbed up and down. She'd missed the ocean. She'd missed this place.

Suddenly a head bobbed up in front of her. It was all she could do not to slam into his very muscular and trim body.

"Shit," she said, "are you trying to make me have a stroke?"

A grin spread across his handsome face. "It's not safe to swim alone. I'm here to rescue you, if you need me."

"Ha-ha! If I try to stand up, my toes will touch the sand," she said. "I'm hardly in any danger. The only danger around me is you. I have a mean punch that I'm not afraid to use."

"Who pissed in your cereal this morning?"

"It's evening. I don't eat cereal. Have you ever heard it's not nice to surprise someone like that?"

"Yeah, but it's kind of fun," he said. "Especially when they jump like you did."

She gave him the stink eye she used on her kids and he grinned at her.

She began to swim to the shore again and he followed alongside her.

"You're in good shape," he said. "Better than most of the women I know."

It was all she could do to keep from saying *don't notice my physical shape*, not because she was ashamed but rather she didn't want him gazing at her body. She didn't want him thinking they were going to start up again. Twenty-six years had passed. Long enough for her to know better.

No. Just no. Men were dangerous. Not only to her body but to her psyche. She didn't need this right now, maybe never. Right now, she was concentrating on finishing the house before her children arrived.

"Thank you, we had a swimming pool with our home and I used it all the time," she said remembering how after the children had grown up, she was basically the only one who swam in the beautiful pool.

"Sounds like you enjoyed it," he said.

"Dr. Plastic Dick didn't swim because he didn't want his skin out in the sun, but yet he…"

Like a slam to the gut, it hit her. Son of a bitch, he didn't play golf. He just told her he was going to play the game and yet she'd found no receipts from the club where he played. He had no golfer's tan, nothing. That's when he and Lustful Lily spent time flying off together somewhere.

The private jets.

Staring at her, he frowned. "Bad memory?"

"Yeah," she said laughing. "I just realized he would tell me he was going to play golf, but he was really dallying with Lustful Lily."

"You must really hate him," he said.

She thought about it. Whatever love she'd felt for Ryan had died when she learned where his heart attack occurred. But did she hate him? Would she really spend that much energy and emotion on him?

"Maybe not hate," she said. "Definitely not love, just an extreme sense of frustration that he did this for five years and I never realized. All the time, I thought he was just a dedicated doctor when really he was just a dedicated cheater. Makes me feel really stupid."

"You're not stupid," he said to her. "Not by any means."

She wondered what he would think if she ever told him about their child. Wouldn't *he* feel stupid then?

They swam in a little closer to the beach and then walked out and lay on the beach towels on the sand.

Lying there, she realized he never told her anything about his life.

"Why do we always talk about me?"

"Because your situation is so interesting," he said. "Mine was just a cheating wife who finally decided it was time to leave. Really kind of boring."

"You consider cheating boring?" she asked, raising her brows to stare at him.

Shaking his head, she could see the hurt in his dark brown eyes.

"No, but when you're doing it with your boss, it's kind of easy to spot," he said. "She wasn't very creative at hiding her affair. Honestly, I think she wanted to get caught. Your husband seemed to be much better at hiding his affair."

As much as she wanted to disagree, she knew it was true.

The sun heated her skin and dried the saltwater on her very quickly. Ryan would have been screaming sunscreen. Ryan would not be on the beach.

"I'm not certain my husband was creative or if I was just walking around in a mommy fog of some kind. I should have noticed that he was always gone, and yet sometimes, I was glad he wasn't around. Life was easier when he was at work."

Over the last month, she had examined their marriage very carefully. Trying to figure out what she'd done wrong. Her biggest mistake was not being observant. Not checking up on him. Not verifying that he was telling her the truth. She'd been way too trusting.

She needed to stop thinking about him. He was dead and no longer mattered. Time to move on. Ryan was the past and Jennifer was determined to focus on the future. Her future.

When she got the time, she was going to find out how many hours she needed to get her master's degree.

Some children ran past them, dashing into the water,

splashing, and she smiled. They were so young and innocent. She missed her children being that age. She missed her daughter's mischievous smile and her son's big personality.

Oh, how she wished she'd brought them here when they were small, but her family situation had always been tense. After the pregnancy, she had distanced herself from her mother, blaming her for making her give up Madison.

Suddenly she remembered his daughters had come to visit him.

"What are you doing out here? Shouldn't you be entertaining your girls?"

A frown appeared on his face. "They only came for the weekend. They'll be back later this summer, but for now, they're driving to see their mother. I worry about them. I wish they would spend the summer with me. I'd let them move in with me, if they would."

Jennifer smiled. "I can understand that feeling. I miss my kids so much. It's only been a week since I saw Alex and a month for Taylor, but still I need them."

He nodded his head. "Agree."

Homesickness overwhelmed her and she knew that tears were not far behind. She didn't want him to see her cry. She didn't want to cry any more tears.

"I'm going back in," she said, standing and running into the water.

He was right behind her and he swam past her, farther out. Then he did what he always tried to pull on them when they were kids. She appreciated that he was trying to lighten the mood, but still his actions were corny.

"Ugh," he cried. "It's got my leg. He's taking me under."

Shaking her head, she waited. Finally, he gave up and popped back up, clearing the water from his face. As much as she wanted to avoid him, as much as she tried to discourage him, there was an easiness between them. It was like they picked right back up where they were before, so many years ago.

An easiness she'd never felt with Ryan.

But this time there were secrets between them he didn't know about. Secrets that she realized would make him furious with her. Secrets that even she needed to understand better.

"You know, I thought you would grow out of that crazy stunt. It still doesn't work," she told him, her memory flooded with the days they had spent on this beach together. Their laughter, the fun, the pranks they'd pulled, as a group of kids hanging out on the beach.

Those two summers were the best of her life. They were filled with fun, laughter, and playing, until the night of the party.

The party where they had gotten into trouble.

Memories were beginning to crowd into her mind and into her heart. No, no, and no.

She'd just buried a husband. A cheating husband. There was no room in her life for any man.

A grin spread across his face. "My girls thought it was stupid as well."

"Smart ladies," she said, wondering if his girls looked like him or their mother. A pang of jealousy hit her as she thought of his life without her. She should have been his first wife and now she would never be his partner.

Never.

Moving toward the shore, she knew she needed to get away. They had spent too much time together and she wasn't ready for anything more. As much as she didn't love Ryan, she was dealing with the death of a marriage. The death of a belief that he had loved her and their family, only to learn it was all a big lie.

Right now, she needed time to heal. Time to learn to trust again.

"Where are you going," he asked.

"Home," she said. "The sun is setting and I'm going home to read a book."

"What book are you reading," he asked, following behind her.

Was he being just like a child trying to keep her from leaving him?

"A murder mystery about a woman who kills her cheating husband," she said, hoping to maybe frighten him away.

Laughter rumbled from his chest. "I'm reading a psychology book on women."

"Lot of depth there," she said.

"Not really," he said. "Just a lot of psychobabble."

She grabbed her towel and her swimsuit coverup and quickly slipped it over her bathing suit.

"Same time tomorrow," he asked.

A pang of pure pain hit her chest. Whirling around, she shook her head. That was what they always said to one another when they were leaving. Then he would walk her up the beach to her home and kiss her good-bye.

That wasn't happening.

"Depends on how much I get done," she said. "The tile man is arriving tomorrow and I'll be painting the kitchen."

"Are we still on for dinner Thursday night?"

With a sigh, she knew they needed to clear the air. They both had questions, but she also needed to decide if she would tell him about Madison. That was a decision that weighed heavily on her.

A decision she didn't know how to handle. What did you say to a man who obviously didn't know he had a child with her?

"Yes," she said. "I'll see you on Thursday."

"See you then," he said and he didn't walk her up the beach to her house.

Relief filled her. While she enjoyed Dylan's company, she refused to get attached to any man. This wasn't going to happen. She needed time to grieve the death of not only her husband, but her beliefs in her marriage.

CHAPTER 15

Yesterday, she and the tile man had removed all the old formica in the kitchen. She'd helped him remove the tile in the bathrooms and then painted both bathrooms and the kitchen.

Now, Thursday, she could hardly move, but the house was beginning to feel different. Today, the men came and installed the new flooring downstairs and she ordered more for the upstairs. While she did her best to stay out of their way, she had gone upstairs and began the destruction on the rooms.

Curtains were down and in the trash and bedspreads were tossed. She'd gone through the rooms and made a note of what new furniture to buy. Her old bedroom suit she was keeping. It was ratan and she took it apart and carried each piece outside where she spray painted it white erasing the dingy aged yellow.

The floor people would be back tomorrow to finish and so would the tile guy. Tomorrow she would begin to paint the guest bedrooms. Thank goodness the house had four rooms with beds and a bathroom upstairs, plus, a master bath and a half bath for guests.

When this was all finished, she hoped the house would be warm and friendly and a perfect gathering place for her children. It would never compare to their home in Beverly Hills, but it would at least have an open, airy feel about it.

More than anything, she wanted the house to be filled with love.

Pulling on a summery dress, she put on some lipstick and brushed her hair. She was letting it get long. No more fancy haircuts in the Hollywood salon she visited. No more facials or even nail visits.

At least not until she finished the house. Not until she made a decision about whether or not to get a job or return to school. But this first summer, she was going to get her life in order before she committed herself to a company or even school.

This was her healing time. Her magical time to recreate the beach house and banish the secrets of her life.

A time to let go of Ryan forever.

Carrying her sandals down the stairs, she picked up her purse just as the doorbell rang.

Shaking her head, she knew he had come to pick her up.

Opening the door, she gazed at him standing there wearing a Hawaiian shirt and shorts. "Are you ready?"

A little gray was sprinkled throughout his brown hair, but it only made him more attractive. And no matter what, he still had that same sexy voice that always touched her deep inside and sent tingles rippling up her spine.

Damn, it was going to be a long evening.

"Yes, I thought I was going to meet you there," she said.

He grinned, that mischievous smile that she'd fallen for when she was sixteen years old.

With a shrug, he said, "I thought we'd walk down the beach together."

They were going to the same restaurant she'd met her friends. It was the favorite place in town for seafood on the water.

"Let's go," she said. "You do realize this is not a date."

Maybe that was cold, but she had to make certain he understood.

"Yes," he said. "You hate men. I hate women. We're just two friends who have some unfinished business."

She didn't respond, wanting to wait until she was sitting across from him, with a glass of wine in her hand. And no, she was not going to drink too much tonight. For this discussion, she needed her wits about her.

And she was still undecided about whether or not to tell him about Madison. Jennifer wanted to meet her first.

"Can I hold your hand?" he asked.

"No," she responded.

"I just wanted to make certain you didn't trip or fall in the sand," he said.

"Understand, but I'm very capable of walking," she replied, setting limits. Hard limits.

No hand holding, no kissing, no hugs, nothing that signaled a growing attraction.

If people saw them walk up to the restaurant holding hands, tongues would be wagging. As it was, they were probably going to wag anyway. But she didn't care. This could not even resemble a date.

Even though she liked Dylan, she wasn't ready to jump into a relationship with him. She couldn't.

When they reached the door, she could see the restaurant was busy.

"We have reservations," Dylan said and she raised her brows at him.

The man had made reservations, so they wouldn't have to wait. That was thoughtful of him.

The waitress led them through the throng of diners to a seat with an ocean view. The restaurant didn't have windows, but rather awnings that were pulled down at night. He pulled out her chair and she sank down and glanced at the rolling sea. The sun was just beginning to fade and she could see a sailboat out on the water, bobbing up and down on the waves. She loved the rocking motion of a boat.

A nice breeze blew in off the water and sea gulls screeched as they searched the beach for a snack.

They ordered drinks and glanced through the menu.

"I'm buying my dinner," she said.

"No, you're not," he replied, not even looking at her.

"This is not a date," she said.

"No, it's not. It's two old friends catching up."

"Friends don't buy each other's dinner," she said, knowing it was a lie.

"You need better friends," he told her, laughing.

The waitress came over and took their orders. After he told her what he wanted, he smiled at the girl and said, "When we're done, bring the check to me."

"You're a pain in the ass," she said.

"God, I love it when you talk dirty to me," he said and the waitress started to laugh, then quickly walked away.

"Now that, that is settled, I have some questions," he said. "Why didn't you answer my letters?"

Taking a sip of wine, she stared into his beautiful dark eyes. "I never received letters from you. Why didn't you answer my letters? In fact, why didn't I ever hear from you again?"

Shaking his head, he frowned. "I didn't receive any of your letters. Were they returned?"

"No," she said, remembering how she had written him and put the letter on the cabinet for her mother to mail. Trusting her to make certain it was sent.

Maybe that was the problem, she'd put her trust in her mother.

"Neither were mine," he said.

They sat there a moment.

"You didn't answer my calls either," he replied. "Was that on purpose?"

"You never called," she said and then she stopped. "Did you call the house phone?"

"Yes, the beach house number," he said. "What happened? I looked for your Dallas number but it wasn't listed."

It all seemed to be coming together.

"My mother kept telling me not to get involved with

you. That I was too young for a serious boyfriend. I blew her off. Then suddenly out of the blue with no warning, my parents woke me up early one morning and told me we were leaving the island. If I remember right, it was the end of July."

By then she was having morning sickness and her breasts were tender.

"Yes, it was," he said. "Because my parents stayed until the middle of August and then we returned to Santa Fe."

She should tell him why they left, but she couldn't. Not here. Not now. It wasn't until they arrived home that her mother confronted her with her suspicions.

"We returned to Dallas and spent the rest of the summer in town. I thought you didn't care and that's why I never heard from you."

"That wasn't it at all. I thought you'd abandoned me," he said.

An eerie feeling overcame her and she felt sad. By her mother stopping her letters from being mailed and her possibly blocking his number, she had kept them apart. In the most trying time of her life, her mother kept her from Dylan and he had never learned of her pregnancy.

"I don't know for certain, but I think… I gave my mother my letters to mail to you, which was really dumb."

Looking down at his hands wrapped around his wine glass, his eyes snapped up to look into hers.

"So you didn't just ignore my letters?"

"No. When you called, did you leave me a message?"

"Yes, with your mother who always answered," he said, slowly nodding. "You broke my teenage heart."

And hers.

"I'm sorry. My heart was broken too. I thought you didn't want anything else to do with me. And after everything, I was devastated."

He glanced out at the ocean. "Your mother was right. We were young."

"Yes," she said softly not wanting him to ruin what they had so many years ago.

"But damn it, I cared for you. I loved you and when you left and didn't return my calls, it nearly killed me."

Maybe she should tell him about Madison, but not here, not like this. And she knew without a doubt, he would be angry.

Oh, how life could have been so different if he'd known about the baby. Her chest tightened with pain as she thought of how she'd waited to hear from him. And there were no calls. No letters. Nothing from Dylan.

"I felt the same," she said softly. "After that summer, I focused on school and didn't date until I was a senior in college. And not long after that, I met Ryan."

He reached across the table and took her hand. "What we had felt so real. More real than anything I ever experienced afterward. Even more real than what I had with my wife. Maybe I was young and innocent, but it felt like a forever kind of love."

Tears welled in her eyes. If only he knew what happened.

"Me too," she said, unable to pull her hand away, knowing that what they shared had been real.

"I kept waiting on your calls or letters or even for you to show up in person."

"Believe me, I considered it," he said. "I just wanted to know what happened."

Her mother happened. She'd kept them apart.

Pain clenched her heart as she thought of how she had cried herself to sleep thinking he didn't want her.

With a sigh, he released her hand and leaned back. "Unfortunately, when I couldn't find you, I think I settled. Maria told me our love never felt real to her. I tried to make my marriage work, but she said it seemed fake. Sadly, when she said that to me, I understood."

Looking back, Jennifer wondered if she'd settled with Ryan. He'd been different, protective, and she liked that about him. But had she loved him like she had Dylan?

"How long have you been divorced?"

"Four years," he said. "The girls were in high school and middle school. Now, one is about to start college and the other one is in college. I'm so proud of my daughters, but I think about them when I think about us."

She took another sip of wine, wanting to be clear about what he was thinking. "What do you mean?"

"That night someone spiked the punch at the beach party. We found ourselves behind a sand dune. Things went too far. We were so lucky that night. It was the best night and the worst night, and we could have created a baby."

Here was her opening, her chance, and yet she couldn't get the words out of her mouth. She wanted to meet

Madison before she told him about her. She wanted some time with her daughter alone.

She'd been ripped from her arms and she needed to know her before Dylan learned about her.

Biting her lip, she glanced down and sighed.

"If my mother was alive, I would ask her about the letters and the phone calls, but she's dead," she said.

"Understand," he replied. "Mine passed away about two years ago. Not long after my divorce."

Reaching across the table again, he picked up both of her hands. "I know you're not ready for another relationship. Hell, your husband's only been dead a month. But could we at least be friends? I'm not going to lie to you that I don't feel the same attraction, but we're now adults. We know there are consequences to our actions and I'd just like to be your friend for now."

Relief filled her. While part of her was attracted to him, she knew she was in no emotional shape to start a relationship. And there were still secrets between them. Secrets that could tear them apart.

"Dylan, I would like that very much," she said. "When I came here, I hoped I wouldn't see you, because frankly, I hated you. You'd not returned my calls or letters, and well, I was hurt. But now that I know you tried, I feel different. And in the last week, bumping into you has been fun. For now, I can be your friend, but there is so much I'm still dealing with. My children are my top priority. They have to be."

A grin spread across his face. "Believe me, I understand. My girls are so important to me."

They lifted their wine glasses.

"To being friends," Dylan said.

And Jennifer hoped that once she told him the secret, they would remain friends.

"Friends," Jennifer said as she bumped her glass against his.

CHAPTER 16

Three days later, she gazed around the house at the changes and smiled. The new floors were in and looked stunning, the kitchen had new granite counter tops with turquoise highlights that matched the paint on the walls of the living area.

The backsplash was a lovely tile that matched the countertops. After all the work was done, she realized she really needed to update the appliances. Tomorrow once again, she would go to Corpus Christi and order new appliances and new bedroom furniture.

Next week, the tile guy planned on redoing the bathroom upstairs and then starting on the master bathroom. The downstairs guest bathroom was completed, and today they had delivered the new furniture.

It looked so good with the walls freshly painted. While she was in town, she wanted to find some paintings that would go with the decor and maybe some throw pillows for the new couch.

Tomorrow, she planned on hanging the new gauzy white curtains over the white blinds.

The kids arrived in two weeks, so she was running out of time. But every day, she saw progress, and every day, the place came more alive. Every day, a new coat of paint washed away the desperate atmosphere in the house.

After everything was done, she wanted to hire a landscaper to redo the front lawn. Then she would be finished unless she extended the back deck. It was a thought and she hadn't made the decision yet.

It all depended on how much money she spent. She'd done her best to keep it under twenty thousand, but now she was creeping closer to thirty. But soon, she'd be finished.

This all felt so wonderful and different. She had never done this before and she was enjoying redoing the old house. It kind of made her feel like she was giving herself a makeover.

Pouring herself a glass of wine, she was just about to sit on the patio when the doorbell rang.

She had not seen Dylan since their dinner Thursday night and she really hoped it wasn't him. Right now, she couldn't handle being with him. As much as she had wanted him, now didn't feel like the right time.

There was a huge secret between them that blocked her from getting too close, plus she was still dealing with Dr. Plastic Dick's cheating.

Going to the door, she opened it and a beautiful young woman stood there. Jennifer felt her mouth drop open as she stared into Dylan's eyes, his lashes, and her pointed chin and high cheekbones.

And yet she had Jennifer's emerald eyes. They stood there staring at one another.

"Mrs. Moss?"

"Yes," she said, gasping at the realization that this was the baby she'd given up so many years ago. Stunned at how much she looked like her and Dylan.

Without thinking, she pulled her into her arms. "You must be Madison. You look like your father and me. You're beautiful."

"Yes," the girl said choking up. "I'm Madison Wilson."

So many emotions overwhelmed Jennifer as she clung to the girl she'd been forced to give up. Joy, sadness, and love filled her and she felt the tears slip down her cheeks.

"Come in. I thought you were going to call me before you came," she said immediately wondering if one of the guest rooms was ready for company.

"I…I was afraid you would tell me no," she said. "Your address was on the envelope. I decided to surprise you."

Jennifer pushed back out of her arms and wiped her tears away. "I'm sorry for crying. Not a day has gone by that I haven't wondered about you, worried about you, missed you. Please come in the house. Are you going to stay the weekend?"

The young girl seemed timid and yet Jennifer could see the strength in her eyes.

"That depends. I know I dropped in on you unexpectedly," she said.

"Come in and we can sit out on the deck and get to

know each other and then you can make the decision on whether you want to stay or not," Jennifer said, not wanting to push her, but hoping she would stay.

The girl's long dark hair reminded Jennifer of her own and happiness filled her. The baby she'd lost was here in her little beach house. This child of hers and Dylan's. This baby she'd loved for so long and knew nothing about.

"As you can see, I'm in the process of remodeling the house. It used to belong to my parents and I don't think it's been updated in over twenty years," she said, leading her into the kitchen.

"Would you like a glass of wine? I was just about to sit out on the deck and watch the evening beach goers and the sun set. It's what I do every evening."

"That would be nice," she said.

It felt so good to see her, and Jennifer's heart was overflowing with love. They had missed so many years of being together. And yet, they both needed to tell each other what happened in their lives during those missing years.

Her chest filled with joy as she gazed at her daughter.

"Set your things there on the counter and we'll sit outside," she said, carrying the two glasses of wine.

Her daughter was here. Her long-lost baby girl. Tears brimmed in her eyes.

They each took a seat out on the deck and Jennifer picked up her wine glass and took a sip.

"You said your husband recently passed away. Was he my father?"

A chuckle slipped from Jennifer. "No. Your father is very much alive."

The girl brightened.

"Can I meet him?"

Oh, why hadn't she told Dylan about Madison when she had the chance.

"He doesn't know about you. We've only recently reconnected as friends. In time, I'll be happy to introduce you to him, but first I have to tell him about you."

The girl seemed to nod and accept what she told her.

"I'm glad he's not dead," she said. "It's hard not knowing anything about your parents. It's like there is this missing piece in your life. And you wonder if you act like your birth parents or even if you look like them. You scan people in the mall and wonder if they are your mother."

Jennifer frowned. She'd written a letter to her right after she'd been born, when they'd taken her away from her. What happened to it?

"When they took you away from me, I wrote you a letter. Did you not receive it?"

Madison shook her head. "No. I never received anything from you. It's why I'm here. I need to understand why you gave me up. I needed to see what you look like and what my father looks like. I need to know about medical issues in our family. There are so many questions I have. It's like there is a big gaping hole in my soul that I know nothing about."

Again, tears welled in Jennifer's eyes and she reached out and grabbed her hand.

"I was only seventeen when I had you. No, I didn't want to give you up. You were mine. You were my flesh and blood and I loved you the moment I felt your first kick. My mother gave me no choice. She said I was too young and I could not support you. She insisted that I give you up for adoption. She ripped you from my arms and told me it was for the best. I never forgave her."

The memory of that day tore Jennifer's soul in two and she wiped the tears flowing from her eyes. "Those first few months, I would wake up and imagine I heard you crying. I'd get up and search the room, but you were gone. I was a senior in high school, and as soon as I graduated, I went away to college and never moved back in with my parents. I went on my own and only visited them a couple times a year."

The sound of children chasing one another down the beach reached her ears and she remembered wondering every time she saw a child, if that was her daughter.

"What about my father?"

How could she describe Dylan to her? "We were young, but so very much in love. His family had a beach house here and mine had this house. That summer was the second summer we'd been together. He was from Santa Fe, New Mexico. Every day, we played in the ocean with the other teenage kids on the island. Our relationship was so easy going, and I thought that's how all couples were. Little did I know the love we had was special."

Little did she know how difficult marriage was until she married Ryan. And their love had never been like what she had with Dylan.

"One night in June, we went to a party on the beach. We were all there, dancing to the music, playing volleyball, and roasting hot dogs. Except someone spiked the punch, and soon, I began to feel so good. We were laughing and giggling and just having fun. Your father is a huge tease, we laughed and played, and he pulled me behind a sand dune."

The memory of their first attempt at lovemaking filled her with a warmth she'd forgotten. Two eager teenagers fumbling and awkward and so carried away by passion, they didn't understand.

"We'd spent time kissing, but never done more than that. That night, there behind that sand dune, you were conceived. Afterward, we lay there and just looked up at the stars and enjoyed being in each other's arms. For a girl's first experience, it was wonderful."

They had been so tempted to do it again, but they both feared what would happen, only problem was she was already pregnant and they didn't know. Over the next few weeks, they had grown closer and closer and she felt certain they would never part.

In her mind, they were one and she imagined them marrying.

"About four weeks later, I started having morning sickness. With all my pregnancies, I experience morning sickness very early. My mother was so worried, she thought I had caught a virus. But it came every morning."

At first, she'd refused to believe she was pregnant. This couldn't happen to her. If they had not been tipsy drunk, she would not have had sex with Dylan, but they had.

She remembered feeling panic, but then she would convince herself, she couldn't be. They had only done it once.

"About two weeks later, my breasts were so tender to

the touch and I had missed my period. I was beginning to get scared and planned on talking to your father about what I was starting to suspect."

This was the part of the story that left her angry and hurt and so damn sad. Life had ripped them apart.

"And then one morning my parents woke me up very early after they had loaded the car. We went home three weeks early. They did not give me a chance to say good-bye to my friends. They did not give me a chance to tell Dylan good-bye. They yanked me out of bed and we returned to Dallas."

Madison took a sip of her wine. "Did my father contact you?"

"He tried. I tried. But my parents must have interfered. They must have intercepted his letters. I wrote him and he never received my letters. It was like suddenly he dropped off the face of the earth and I was expecting his child."

Remembering those days, she took a sip of wine. They had been gut wrenching. Oh, how she had wanted him to ride in and save her and the baby, but he didn't.

"They kept me in the house. My mother kept talking to me about college, and how I had to keep my grades up so I could get a scholarship. The only time I left the house was to go to a doctor's appointment. It was the most disheartening time of my life. It was during this time, I began to hate my mother."

A cool breeze blew off the ocean and she recalled the night she went into labor. How she walked across the room and her water broke. "On the night you were born, I was so thrilled. You were beautiful. You were perfect and I was going to keep you. Only my mother had other plans for you. She told me a family had been chosen. That I could see you whenever I wanted to, but it was a big lie."

"And that's when she took me from your arms," Madison asked quietly.

"Yes," Jennifer said, tears running down her face. "You were always wanted. I loved you so very much and I even tried to find you when I was young. I could never find them. I was given false names and fake phone numbers. I searched for you, but you were gone."

It had been gut wrenching to turn up one dead end after another. So painful, she'd finally given up.

"Later, I decided you didn't know me and it would not be right to take you from the people who loved and took care of you. To disrupt your young life would have been so selfish, regardless of how much it hurt me."

It had been the hardest decision of her young life.

Madison gazed out at the ocean. "They're good people and I love them. They're my mom and dad, but I had to fill this hole in my soul. I had to know about my real mother and father."

Jennifer tried to imagine what her daughter must feel but could only experience her own pain.

"I'm glad to hear you love them and they treated you right," Jennifer said. "You have a half-sister and a half-brother. When the time is right, I'd like to introduce you to them. They've been through a lot this year with the sudden death of their father. And they have no idea you exist."

There would be so much to tell them when they

arrived, but she refused to have secrets between them any longer. It was time they learned the truth.

Madison nodded. "I'd like to meet them."

"Tell me about yourself. Are you out of college?"

A slow smile spread across Madison's face. "Yes and no. I'm going to law school."

Happiness filled Jennifer. "That was my dream to go to law school, but life got in the way. I married Ryan and got pregnant almost immediately. How much more schooling do you have left? Are you married?"

Madison glanced at her. "One more year of law school and then I graduate. Afterward, I'll have to take the bar exam. I'm engaged, but I don't know. You said something that struck a note with me. We struggle and he was insistent I find you. But our relationship is not easy by any means."

"I've had two serious relationships and if it doesn't come easy, walk away. It's not meant to be," she said softly.

Jennifer did not want to interfere. With her children, she had made the decision that she would let them live their lives and never be that overbearing mother who ripped the baby from her arms.

But still, she wanted Madison to be happy. She wanted her children to be happy.

"Come on, let's walk down the beach. I'll show you the sand dune where you were conceived. If ever you need a place to get away, all you have to do is call me and let me know you're coming."

Laughter came from Madison. "That sounds weird. I'm sorry I didn't call this time, but I was afraid you'd say no."

Jennifer shook her head. "You're my daughter. I know you have another family, but if possible, I would love to add you to our lives. Even your mother and father. They will always be your first family, but I'd love to be your second family. No matter what, you'll always be my daughter."

Madison smiled and reached out and hugged her. "I've been so angry that you gave me up. I couldn't imagine how anyone could do that, but now I see. Now I know what happened and now I wonder how you lived with the knowledge all these years."

Jennifer's heart clenched with pain and joy.

Dear God, this was what she'd wanted to hear for so many years. No one had ever understood her side. Not her mother. Not her father, no one. Now she had her daughter back and the empty hole in her soul was being replenished.

This day would always be reconciliation day. Almost like a birthday.

And soon she had to tell Dylan the truth. Soon. Very soon.

As they stepped off the deck and down toward the ocean, Barbara came running out of her house in her old lady smock.

"Jennifer? Is that your daughter?"

She was not going to deny her. This was a time of healing.

"Yes, Barbara this is Madison," she said.

"She's the spitting image of you. Beautiful. When is all that construction noise going to stop? What are you doing, rebuilding the house?"

"Just about," she said, halting in front of the woman. "The tile man is working on the bathrooms now and after that I'll be done with the inside except to finish painting."

Shaking her head, Barbara frowned. "Your mother loved that house. She'd be so upset to learn you're redecorating."

Oh, good grief. If the woman only knew how bad the inside had been.

"You're right, she would have," Jennifer said. "But she's not here and it hasn't been done in over twenty years. It was due. Now if you'll excuse me, we're going to go for a walk down the beach."

Hurrying down the boardwalk, the two of them laughed. "She's a crabby old lady, but she's also very nice. And she has no one."

Jennifer knew she had to look out for Barbara. The woman needed her.

"I wish I'd met your mother," Madison said. "Sounds like she was quite the character. Strong and resilient."

Oh, her mother was definitely the stronger parent, the more domineering one, the person she hated because of what she'd done.

"When we get back, I'll show you pictures of her," Jennifer said, thinking she needed to see the family she'd never met. The family she belonged to.

"When can I meet my father?" Madison asked.

"Soon. I need to talk to him first because he doesn't know about you and I think he's going to be very angry."

CHAPTER 17

Madison spent the weekend and Jennifer fell even more in love with her daughter. She was smart, beautiful, and had a kind soul that reminded her so much of Dylan. She liked to tease and laugh and the girl even sounded like Dylan.

Jennifer could see parts of herself and Dylan in her and her heart swelled with love. But how would Dylan take the news?

All the years of being apart were torture, and yet since this weekend, she couldn't wait to introduce her first daughter to her children.

This morning, she had gotten up the courage and called Dylan. She told him they needed to talk. He was due at her house at any moment and her nerves were racing like they were on fire.

Would he accept Madison or would he hate Jennifer for not telling him sooner?

Deep in her heart, she knew he was going to be furious

with her, and yet she'd done everything she could think of to reach him.

The doorbell rang and she knew tonight was going to be rough. He would be so mad at her, and she couldn't blame him, but she'd really had no control over the situation.

If she had been in control, that child would never have left her arms.

She went to the door and pulled it open.

He stood there in his Hawaiian shirt with a bottle of wine in his hands. Did he think she was going to tell him she wanted to date?

"Didn't come empty-handed. I thought maybe we had something to celebrate tonight," he said. "You're madly in love with me and can't live without me another second."

She invited him in and then led him into the kitchen where she took down two crystal wine glasses.

"Sorry to disappoint you," she said. "Besides, you hate women and I hate men."

And after tonight, he could possibly hate her as well.

"You're softening me up on the fairer sex," he said. "House looks really nice. I like your changes."

She glanced around and smiled. It was finally all coming together. The new appliances would be delivered on Friday and the last of the new furniture came next Monday.

Her children arrived next Friday to spend the summer with her.

"Thanks, we're getting closer to being finished. Want to sit outside?" she asked. The covered deck on the first floor was her favorite, but the deck outside the landing upstairs was where she liked to sit at night and watch the boat lights travel across the wide expanse of nothing but the ocean.

It was a lonely feeling watching the lights, but she enjoyed it very much.

"Let's go," he said.

They walked outside and sank down in the lounge chairs she'd found at a local second-hand store and repainted.

"This house always had the best view of the beach and the ocean," he said, grinning at her. "It's hard to believe it's been twenty-six years since that summer."

This was her opening and yet she was so afraid of what this would do to their friendship.

She picked up her wine glass and took a big guzzle. This was so hard.

"There is something you should know about that summer," she said quietly, hating this information, but knowing it wasn't fair to her daughter not to let her meet her father.

"We talked about that party we went to and we had sex back behind the sand dune. Someone had spiked the punch and we were both a little drunk," she said quietly. "Then six weeks later, my parents woke me up in the early hours of the morning and whisked me back to Dallas."

A frown appeared on his face and she could see his brown eyes gazing at her with a worried expression.

"Yes, I never saw you again," he said, his face growing solemn. "You never received my letters and I never received yours. You said your mother kept us apart, but you never said why."

She just needed to tell him. Taking a deep breath she blurted out the words.

"I was pregnant," she said. "Every day, I grew more suspicious as my body changed. But I wasn't certain until after we were home and my mother took me to the doctor. I was pregnant."

Dylan slowly rose from his chair and began to pace the patio area. He ran his hand through his hair.

"Why didn't you call me?"

"I tried to," she said. "I thought you were avoiding me."

Slowly his face changed and she could see him growing angry.

"That was my child. I had a right to know," he said.

"Agree," she said softly. "I wrote you and told you about the baby. For months, I hoped you would drive up and whisk me away. But you didn't come. I didn't hear from you. You disappeared."

His face contorted with rage. "You were the one that disappeared. I was right here."

"I know," she said softly.

Glaring at her, he said, "People don't just disappear. You should have found someone to get in touch with me. I would have come for you."

"I wasn't allowed to talk to any of my friends from here. Mother didn't want anyone to know I had a bun in the oven."

Sinking down onto the chair, he covered his face with his hands. "Damn it, Jennifer, you should have found some way to get in touch with me. That was my child too. What did you do?"

With a sigh, she took a gulp of wine.

"I wanted to keep the baby. If I had kept the baby, I planned on getting in touch with you. But after she was born, I was holding her, telling her how much I loved her when my mother told me it was time."

She gulped knowing how much she hated telling this story.

"Time for what?"

"She took the baby from my arms and told me a family had been found. A good family who would raise the child. I could see her anytime I wanted, and she even gave me their name and phone number."

Tears filled in her eyes. She didn't want to cry in front of him, she didn't want to let him see her pain.

"Again, she lied to me. After that day, I never saw her. I never found her, even though I looked. I was going to get my daughter back. That family name was bogus."

Hate for her mother and what she'd done filled her with anguish. So much time had been lost between the three of them.

"We're going to find her," he said.

She took a deep breath and slowly released it.

"The day that Ryan died, I received a letter from her. She found me," she said.

His head yanked up and he glared at her. "And?"

"She was here this weekend," she said.

A roar escaped his throat and he glared at her. "And you didn't tell me. It's bad enough I don't know about her for twenty-five years, but she was here and you didn't bring her to see me. I have a right to know my child. She's mine too."

Now he was furious.

"I didn't know she was coming. She just showed up on my door."

"You know how to find me," he yelled.

For a moment, she wondered how much the neighbors could hear. Dylan was obviously upset.

"Call me selfish, but I wanted to get to know her. She asked about you and she wants to meet you. But I told her not until I told you about her."

"Damn it, Jennifer. I've lost twenty-five years with her," he said. "And I blame you. You should have tried harder to find me. To contact me."

At seventeen, she'd been terrified, scared, and she wanted to find him. But he hadn't answered her phone calls. He hadn't answered her letters and she didn't know how to reach him.

"Why is it all my fault? I tried. God, how I tried to reach you and you never returned my phone calls or my letters. I needed to speak to you. To tell you I was pregnant and alone and scared to death. But you didn't answer your phone."

Glaring at her, he said, "I never received one of those calls. Not one. I would have been there by your side. There is no way I would have turned my back on you or our baby."

Tears rolled down her face. The past was the past and there wasn't a damn thing they could do to change it.

"She's coming back this weekend and I told her I would introduce the two of you," she said.

He set his wine glass on the table and stood.

"I'm so angry right now, I can't think straight. Later, when I get home, maybe the rational part of me will return, but for now, I've got to get out of here." Shaking his head, he glared at her. "We have a daughter together. A daughter you have kept secret for half my life. Damn it, Jennifer. Damn it. You could have told me the other night. You could have told me years ago and you didn't."

"And this is why I decided not to tell you. I knew you would react this way in a crowded restaurant. The whole town would have known we have a daughter when you jumped up and left."

"Your damn right they would have," he said. "She's my child too."

Suddenly he stepped off the deck and walked toward the beach.

That had gone exactly how she feared it would. Exactly.

Once again, it was all her fault. Men were all the same. They never seemed to accept responsibility for the chaos they created in a women's world.

Stupidly, she thought they might have a chance again. But no, she was done with men.

CHAPTER 18

The sun had sunk below the western horizon and a cool breeze blew off the ocean. A fire was burning in the pit down the way from the house, and Jennifer had cooked hot dogs, burned marshmallows, and now was ready to begin tonight's ceremonies as her friends sipped on their wine.

Since Madison's father now knew about her, it was time for all secrets to be revealed. The reason why she had never returned to Mustang Island, her secret pregnancy, and her recently returned daughter.

She had drunk just enough wine to give her courage.

"There's something I need to tell you," she told her friends after her third glass of wine.

She had invited them all over for a photo-burning party. This morning, she'd needed a break from painting after the can of white ran dry. She'd have to make another damn trip to the hardware store and she didn't really want to go. Since the argument with Dylan, she'd been down.

Really down. More so than after Ryan's death and subsequent funeral.

Damn, Dylan. He had no idea of the pressure she'd been under at so young an age. God, how she had tried to reach him, but he didn't understand.

Today, she'd unpacked more boxes and gone through all the photos.

Each child had their own box of photos that included wedding photos, most of their baby pictures, and even pictures of her parents. Madison had her own box. It included pictures of her and Dylan from their teenage years. She'd forgotten all about the photos until she found them and she no longer wanted them. They were a reminder of that summer she'd fallen in love with him.

Screw him.

"I've decided that I hate men. All of them," she said, knowing she was drunk but not caring. "Every last stinking one of them."

"Even Dylan," Amanda asked.

"Right now, especially Dylan," she said and they all perked up, their eyes widening.

"Oh dear God, she slept with him," Nicole said. "We all knew it was going to happen sooner or later."

Jennifer turned on her. "Uh, uh, uh," she responded. "Yes, I slept with him, but it was twenty-six years ago. I'm not going anywhere near that dick. It's dangerous."

There was a gasp and then they started giggling. Maybe they had all consumed way more wine than was needed.

"Good for you," Crystal said. "I hope you enjoyed every minute of it. A woman needs pleasure."

Her words stunned her and she felt a tear gather in her eye.

"It was good," she said. "Damn good. Unfortunately, it's the reason I left here without saying good-bye."

For the next ten minutes, she told them what happened while she continued to sip wine. Tonight, she needed that wine. She deserved that alcohol. Life had been so tough these last few months. Dylan's reaction was the final betrayal, and right now, she was on the edge.

"You gave up a baby?" Amanda said, the mother of five who probably would never understand how this could happen to Jennifer.

If she judged her, it might destroy their friendship because Jennifer felt so sensitive to everything. The least little thing would have her in tears. The least little thing and she would come up fighting. She was tired of being the kicked dog.

"My mother ripped that sweet, precious child from my arms," she said quietly. "I didn't want to give her up. I wanted to be that single mother who somehow succeeded in life. But I wasn't given that chance."

"Damn," Crystal said. "Your mother always was a bitch."

"Yes," Jennifer said with a little laugh. "But Dylan thinks I could have found a way to get to him. Hell, I couldn't even get to any of you, to let you know what happened to me. The only way I could have reached him was by carrier pigeon."

"You've told him," Nicole said.

"Yes, and he was so angry. Back then, I wanted him to ride in on a white horse and save me. I wanted him to know I was pregnant. He never received my letters and yet he's angry. I thought he had abandoned me."

Just remembering those thoughts made her angrier at his reaction.

Nicole stood. "By Texas law, you are required to let the father know he has a child."

Jennifer threw another log on the fire and a shower of sparks rose up in the air. "Then my mother should be in jail. I tried. And now he hates me."

Why his anger hurt her so badly, she didn't understand, but it did. All she had wanted at that time in her life was to speak to him to tell him what was happening. To marry him and live happily ever after.

"What happened to the baby?" Amanda asked.

"My mother arranged a private adoption. She's now twenty-five and recently I received a letter from her. She spent the weekend with me." Tears gathered in her eyes. "It's so great to see her again. That's why I told Dylan about her. She wants to meet him."

For a moment, there was silence. Nicole shook her head. "Dear God, men can be so obtuse sometimes. You would have wanted him to know about her. Knowing you, it's a wonder you didn't hop on a bus to go find him."

"I tried," she said, remembering the day her mother locked her in the house.

"I was hoping you two would get back together," Crystal said. "He's a good man. You guys always made such a cute couple."

Cute couples didn't mean the marriage or relationship

would always be happy. It took more to make a marriage work. A lot more.

Jennifer walked to the table and poured herself another glass of wine. She didn't want to think about Dylan. And there was no way in hell they were ever getting back together. Cuteness or not.

"Would you have gotten back with him?" Amanda asked.

Why were they asking these questions? It was over. Dead, gone, and buried. Just like her husband.

"My husband has only been in the ground two months. I'm not ready to consider another man. Especially one who hates me."

But her heart knew she was lying. She'd thought about Dylan. Especially after their dinner the other night. Not now. Maybe in time. But now it was never. He hated her and she didn't really like him much right now either.

"Damn, I hoped in six months to a year, we'd be going to the wedding we've been waiting years for."

"No," she said. "I'm that lying bitch who didn't contact him and tell him about his child. He hates me."

Amanda got up and pulled her in for a hug. The mother of five seemed to have accepted that she'd given up a child against her will.

"You've had a tough year," she said.

Oh no, those were the kind of words that would have her crying. She didn't want to cry in front of her friends. She was tired of crying.

Crystal came up and joined in the hug. "You have every reason to hate men. They've really done you wrong."

Oh no, the tears were bubbling to the surface.

Nicole got up and joined in the hug. "Maybe it's time we went over and kicked Dylan's ass. Maybe it's time we showed him that our girl did not do this by choice. Maybe it's time we let him know he was the jerk who got you pregnant. All he had to do was use a condom."

"It broke," Jennifer said, hysterical laughter bubbling with tears. "We were out behind a sand dune and the damn rubber broke. There is no telling how long he carried it in his billfold. One good push and it was done."

She laughed so hard, she feared she was going to pee her pants. "While he was trying to get the condom out of his billfold, he dropped it in the sand and it took us forever to find it. It was hot, we were sweaty, sand was in every crack and yet somehow we made a baby that night. We were young and stupid and someone spiked the damn punch."

"Sounds like a perfect first time," Nicole said. "Better than mine."

"It wasn't bad," Jennifer said. "Out under the stars with the sound of the ocean, we were both a little tipsy; it was nice."

"Oh, I remember that party," Crystal said. "The girls on the beach had a wet T-shirt party and you weren't there. We were all drunk on the punch."

Amanda sighed. "You weren't the only one to get pregnant at that party. That's when Eric and I hooked up for the first time. We didn't mean to, but the alcohol and the night just seemed to get away from us. We didn't use a condom and I got pregnant."

Jennifer glanced at her friend. "Damn, Amanda, I didn't know. Both of us on the same night."

"How could you know? You were gone. My parents forced Eric to marry me and here we are twenty-six years later with five kids."

"The sex must be really good," Crystal said.

"The sex was good. Really good, but lately, it's kind of boring. It's like his mind is somewhere else and not on me or the kids."

In the firelight, Amanda looked sad. Jennifer remembered that feeling of her husband's interest was anywhere but on her. Good reason to never marry again. Every time she felt sad, she should remember that experience of Ryan not noticing her. Of Dylan accusing her.

"Damn, I guess I'm just glad I was there for the wet T-shirt contest. Which, if I remember right, Crystal won," Nicole said giggling.

"Winner, winner chicken…oh shit," Crystal said. "You guys have gotten married I'm still a three-time engagement loser."

"I'm not married," Nicole said. "Sometimes I wonder if I'm a lesbian and then I look at you ladies and think, oh hell no. I want to feel a man's chest beneath my fingers. To feel—"

"We get it," Amanda said laughing.

She erupted in giggles and it was like all of them started laughing. One incident at a beach party had caused all of them some kind of grief.

"Come on, time to burn Ryan," she said. "These are

photos that his children either shouldn't see or they're so good, I can't stand to see them."

She started to run around the fire pit, tossing in photos, laughing. "Ryan's medical graduation party. Very boring. A bunch of surgeons standing around talking about whether or not to start their own practice."

Amanda came up behind her and started running around the fire pit with her. "Hand them to me and I'll toss them in."

"Ryan's first day at his new job," she said. "Jerk."

They danced around the fire pit once more and she busted out laughing. "Dick pics."

"What? Let me see," Crystal said.

Nicole came up behind Amanda and put her hands on her waist. "Let's start a Congo line that tosses the photos into the fire."

Crystal came up and joined them. "Damn, I wish Paige was here. She'd be calling up an escort service and getting us all a date."

They turned and glared at her.

"No men, tonight," Jennifer said. "This is the burning of a cheating husband."

Nicole suddenly stopped. "No, we're doing this wrong. We need to write down a wish, something positive, and throw it into the fire."

"True," Crystal said. "Our girl has had a very bad year. It's time to turn it around with positive thinking and love."

"Toss those photos and then let's end it with a wish for good things to happen."

Good grief, did they not understand that this was an

exorcism for her? She was burning the past as much as she could. What did she want for her future? Right now, she was taking it one day at a time. It was all she could handle.

"That's a problem. I don't know what I want in my future," she said and then the image of her children swam before her eyes. All three of them.

"Yes, I know," she said, her heart filling with love. They were the most important aspect in her life. Nothing else mattered.

Amanda ran into the house and came out with a notebook. "Here, all of you write on the paper and then we're going to throw it into the fire. This is a cleansing for all of us. A chance to bring more positivity into our life."

The women retreated into different corners.

"Don't tell anyone," Crystal said. "This is between you and the universe."

Jennifer threw the last of the pictures into the fire and then she grabbed a pen and a piece of paper.

For each child, she wrote a special wish and then she walked over and threw her hopes into the fire.

Then Amanda. Nicole and Crystal did the same.

They stared into the flames.

"I think it's time for more wine," Nicole said. "Ryan has been thoroughly burned and the universe has our positive wishes. Now, let's drink on them."

Amanda stepped back, picked up the last bottle of wine, and poured everyone a drink.

"You ladies do realize it's after midnight," she said giggling. "I haven't been out this late in a long time. Maybe this will help Eric to appreciate me more."

Jennifer sighed. "Normally, I'm in bed long before now."

"Damn, I would really like to snuggle up to someone tonight," Crystal said with a sigh. "I think Aaron is going to ask me to marry him, but the sex is so incredibly boring. What am I going to do?"

"Do you love him?" Jennifer asked.

"He's convenient," she said.

"Not a good answer," Amanda said. "If it's boring now, it will be a real snoozer later when you have five children who get more attention than you do."

Nicole stood. "Amanda, you need to buy the sexiest nightie you can find, maybe some whip cream and some love cuffs. It's time to bring the spark back in your marriage."

She sighed. "Don't you think I've tried that? He rolled over and went to sleep."

"Stop giving him options. Tell that big boy, you're going to spank his ass if he doesn't give his wife some attention," Crystal said.

The women howled with laughter and Amanda shook her head. "I don't think I can do that. I mean, we're a very vanilla couple. He even turned up his nose at the whipped cream."

Suddenly a door across the way slammed shut.

"Jennifer, is that you? You girls are being too loud. Have you been drinking?"

They all snickered.

"Sorry, Barbara," she said. "We're performing an exorcism. Would you like to join us?"

"Dear God in Heaven, a what?"

"We have wine, if you'd like to join us," she said, thinking it was probably the perfect way to get the old lady to shut up. She wasn't ready for the party to end. Tonight, she needed this time with her friends.

The women were shaking their heads no and suddenly Barbara moved across the beach to her deck.

"You girls are drunk," she said.

"Yes, ma'am," Jennifer said. "We burned pictures of my dead husband."

"Why?"

"To exorcism him out of my life," she said, knowing she would not tell this woman the real reason her husband had died. Some people were like megaphones and Barbara gossiped more than anyone Jennifer knew.

"Where's that wine?"

Thank goodness Jennifer had an extra bottle still in the house.

Two hours later after the fire had died out, Barbara had to be helped back to her house.

"Invite me again," she said laughing. "I haven't had that much fun in years. Exorcisms are fun."

The woman had no idea what she was talking about, but Jennifer didn't care, and she was not about to explain it to her because then she would want to know why.

Jennifer smiled. She'd started something that would be hard to stop now. But the old woman had confessed how lonely it was in her house and Jennifer thought that could be her someday.

CHAPTER 19

*L*ast night, Madison had arrived and they sat on the deck talking about her childhood and the man she was engaged to marry.

There were warning signs in the relationship, but then who was Jennifer to talk? She hadn't seen the signs in her own marriage that there was trouble. And even today, life had shown her that she should stay away from men.

Now she wondered how Ryan would have handled the news that she had a child out of wedlock. But somehow she just didn't care. He'd hid so much from her. They both had skeletons in the closet, only he died inside one of his skeletons.

And Dylan…the last few weeks she'd enjoyed spending time with him and talking, but now she'd killed that situation as well. Maybe her friends should nickname her the Man Killer because first her husband died and now Dylan was angry with her about Madison.

Today, Jennifer was going to introduce her to her father and then walk away. They needed this time to get to know one another.

And Jennifer didn't want to see Dylan. She didn't want to sit there all afternoon waiting for Dylan to go off on her once again. This time, she would tell him to back off; she'd done the best she could.

They were sipping the last of their coffee on the deck and watching the morning beach joggers run up and down the beach. A nice breeze blew and Jennifer was at peace. She loved having Madison here with her.

Next week, her other children would arrive and she couldn't wait to spend time with them on the beach.

So far, she had not seen Barbara since that night, but the older woman had really enjoyed being with her friends. She'd never considered that Barbara was lonely, and now she would do her best to include her as much as possible.

"Tell me about my father," Madison said.

"He's a professor at a local college here and also teaches classes online. His parents are dead, he's divorced and has two daughters. So you have two more half-siblings."

"As an only child, I always dreamed of having brothers and sisters and now I have four. Wow."

Jennifer took a sip of her coffee. "We're to meet him at the Lobster Tail, a local restaurant. I'm going to walk you down there, introduce you, and then leave the two of you alone to get to know one another."

Madison's eyes widened. "No. Please, I would really like it if you were with me. At least for this first time."

Her daughter didn't strike her as a person easily intimidated or fearful, so why did she want Jennifer there? With a sigh, she didn't want to stay with Dylan being so angry with her. Since that night, she had not heard from him and it was just as well. She didn't need more drama in her life.

"You have to understand that he's not happy with me right now. We've gone from being friends to him hating me because I didn't tell him about you," she said. "So he probably would prefer if I left."

"Well, I would prefer if you stayed. I don't know him."

"He's your father."

"But I don't know him and my fiancé doesn't want me to be alone with strange men," she said.

The more Jennifer heard about this fiancé the more she didn't like him and she'd never met him before. Or was this just an excuse? But why?

"If you tried to reach him, he has no reason to be angry with you," she said. "You told me you wrote him and he didn't respond."

"I did," Madison said. "I also tried to call him but got no answer. In my young girl's fantasy mind, I wanted him to come get me and marry me. But that never happened."

Madison shook her long dark hair, and Jennifer was amazed at how beautiful this woman was. And she didn't want her to have any misgivings about her father.

And yet she felt like she owed it to her to do what she wanted and needed. It wouldn't always be this way, but for now, she would stay with her.

"All right, but I may decide halfway through to leave," she said. "We went from being the best of friends to stark enemies. He thinks I didn't attempt to contact him. And he's wrong, I did," she said, standing and taking the empty coffee cups inside.

Madison sat outside staring at the ocean.

"This is all so surreal to me," she said. "Meeting both of you. Learning I have four half-siblings. Seeing how much alike we are," she said. "Sometimes I think it's all a dream."

Jennifer could see that it must be overwhelming to have so much thrown at you at once. But, hey, she was the one who sold everything and packed up and moved from Hollywood to Texas.

"Whenever I feel like life is getting to me, I come out here and sit and take deep breaths. That ocean breeze can suck the fear right out of you."

"My parents are worried that they're losing me to you," she said. "But they have been so good to me, I will always be their daughter."

After meeting her daughter, knowing she must continue to share her was so hard. She understood and she would never try to take her away from the people who adopted her and loved her, but still, she was her daughter as well.

"I would love to meet them and tell them thank you," she said. "You will have to balance your life between us. I'll always try to make it easy for you, but I admit to wanting to see you every chance I get, including holidays. I'll accept whatever you choose to share with me."

"Thank you." Madison smiled. "When will I get to meet your children? His children?"

"Soon," Jennifer said. "They arrive next weekend and I'd

like to have a few days to explain to them what is going on. I thought maybe you could return the middle of July and we could have a big cookout and everyone get to know one another. Maybe bring your adopted parents."

It sounded so simple, but for some reason, Jennifer feared it would not be. First, she had to tell Taylor about her father and then inform Taylor and Alex about Madison.

So many secrets suddenly unraveling. How would her children react?

It was so much at once, and she feared Taylor's response. She'd go from the oldest to the middle child and how was that going to sit with her? And her father...she had always been a daddy's girl.

How would she accept that her daddy was a lying cheating man who spent the family fortune?

"I've been thinking about your children and I wonder how they're going to take learning I was the first born. That you gave me up for adoption. I've been wondering if they will accept me into the family."

Jennifer had been thinking the same thing.

"No choice," she said. "You're my daughter just like they're my children. As my mother used to say, suck it up, buttercup."

It was the only saying her mother said that had stuck with Jennifer. The rest she tried to push out of her mind.

"What about Dylan's children?"

"I can't answer that. I've never met them and I know he's very protective of his daughters."

It was not going to be an easy transition.

"But I'm his daughter too," Madison said softly.

"Yes, you are," Jennifer said, thinking she would defend Madison with her dying breath. Dylan would have a fight on his hands if he didn't accept their daughter. She deserved to know her family and her siblings. They may not like it, but Madison was a part of their lives now.

Glancing at her watch, she realized it was time to leave.

"Time to go," she said, standing and picking up her purse.

They walked down the beach, past the lifeguard, the people playing volleyball, and even some seniors relaxing and watching the waves roll in. Children played in the water, their shrill voices a reminder of the fun they were having.

Life was so simple at that age and she hoped that her grandchildren would someday be playing on this beach.

As they approached the restaurant, nerves seemed to attack Jennifer. Since she'd known Dylan, they had always gotten along. This was the first time they'd ever had a serious fight and she didn't know how to react.

"No matter what happens today, I'm thrilled you are back in my life," she told Madison, wanting her to understand she would always be there for her.

"You don't think he will be angry with me?"

"No, it's me he's unhappy with."

Dylan was standing outside the restaurant, watching them approach. As soon as Madison stood before him, he threw his arms around her, his eyes filled with tears.

The expression on his face brought tears to Jennifer's eyes. The man was gut-wrenched and she could see that he loved their daughter immediately.

"If I'd known about you, I would have moved heaven and earth to find you," he said. "You're a part of me and I'm so happy to meet you."

Madison looked a little bewildered.

"Mom couldn't find me," she said.

Jennifer's heart clenched. It was the first time she'd called her mom. And though she knew she had another mom, she welcomed this young woman with all her heart.

"I'm your dad," he said. "Please call me dad."

She pulled back and grinned at him.

He studied her facial features carefully. "You look like my youngest daughter only you have Jennifer's eyes."

A smile spread across her face.

"Let's go eat," he said, wiping his eyes.

Jennifer wanted to walk away, but Madison reached out and took her hand. "Come on, Mom. I want you here with us."

Dylan cut her a quick glance.

"I wanted to let you two have a chance to get to know one another," she said.

"And I want a dinner with both my parents," she said.

Now Jennifer understood. Now she knew what she needed. She needed this time with the two of them to help them bond. She wanted her birth family to have this moment alone. And she couldn't deny her.

"Of course," she said.

Dylan didn't say anything, and she could tell he was still

angry. And she didn't know how to make him realize she'd been duped by her mother. Somehow she hid the phone calls, stopped her letters, done everything she could to keep them apart.

And even today, she was still keeping a wedge between them. Jennifer would always pay the price for her mother's deception. Always.

They sat at a table he'd reserved.

"Mom, says you have two other daughters," she said.

"Yes," he said. "I'm divorced and teach at the local college."

"Tell me about your life," he said, gazing at her.

For the next fifteen minutes, she told him about her childhood and how she'd gone to college and was working toward becoming a lawyer.

He cut a glance at Jennifer. "You know that Jennifer wanted to be a lawyer."

"That's what she told me," Madison said, smiling at her.

Dylan shook his head. "You're all grown up and I feel like I've missed so much."

"Me too," Jennifer said, knowing he would not look at her. "Me too."

Madison smiled. "Mom showed me where I was conceived and told me what happened."

A grin spread across his face. "We were so young and in love. Plus, a little spiked punch helped set the mood. Do you have someone important in your life?"

"Yes," she said. "My fiancé, but I'm having doubts. I don't know. I'm not going to rush into anything. But he did insist that I find my birth parents. And I'm so happy I did."

Shaking his head, Dylan teared up again. "There is so much to tell you. So much to show and introduce you to my other kids."

Reaching across the table, he took her hand. "If I had known, I would have married Jennifer."

A gasp came from Jennifer and she had to look away and wipe the tears that flowed from her eyes.

"Hearing you say that, makes me hate my mother even more," she said softly. "Every night, I dreamed you would show up and whisk me away. That we would somehow go to school and raise our baby. Instead, she took Madison from me."

Dylan reached out and took Jennifer's hand. "I'm sorry I overreacted, but I was so angry. So hurt that something precious had been taken from me. From us."

Her heart seemed to melt and all the love she'd had for him all those years ago flooded her chest. How could she hate this man?

"I'm sorry I never reached you. I tried, oh God, how I tried," she said. "This is what I wanted. What I dreamed about."

There wasn't a dry eye at the table and when the waitress walked up, they shooed her away.

He squeezed her hand hard. "Last night, I realized you would not have kept this information from me. That's not who you are. I let my past experiences cloud what we once had. Can we please go back to where we were?"

Jennifer shook her head. "No," she said, suddenly realizing that was not what she wanted.

Dylan's face sagged with disappointment.

"I know we're older, but I would like to take it really slow and see if we can go back to where we were when we conceived Madison. I want a second chance."

Madison gasped, her eyes twinkling with happiness.

Dylan stood and walked around the table. He pulled her up and took her in his arms and then he kissed her. His mouth covered hers, and though they were in a public restaurant with a room full of people, this kiss felt perfect. Like this was where she belonged.

All the years melted away and the pain of what she'd been through flowed out of a once-closed door as she felt like she'd come home. Like this was where she belonged. This man was her destiny and had always been the one for her.

Clapping hands and hoots and hollering brought her out of the magical place and she pushed back.

Dylan grinned. "I've been wanting to do that since that first day I ran into you at the post office."

She glanced at her daughter as she wiped tears from her eyes. "This makes me so happy. See, Mom, I wanted you to come with me today. Now I have my real family back together."

"Yes," Jennifer said, knowing this felt so right. "But please give me some time. My children don't know you like I do and I don't know how they're going to react."

A smile filled Dylan's face. "We'll take it slow. After this many years, we'll know when it's the right time to take that final step. But for now, let's just enjoy each other and make up for the time we've lost being together. And get to know our daughter."

Madison stood and they all hugged.

The restaurant patrons didn't know what was going on, but they clapped and cheered before they finally settled in.

Jennifer felt a sense of peace unlike anything she'd ever felt before. This was right. This was home.

CHAPTER 20

The next week flew by with the final preparations for the house. Jennifer and Dylan spent as many hours as they could together, talking about the past, the future, and their children. He came over and helped her finish painting the guest bedrooms and hung the curtains she'd bought.

There had been kisses, but they made the decision that they would both know when they were ready to have sex. Until the moment was right, they were waiting.

Right now, Jennifer wasn't ready.

The house was perfect and she felt so proud of it when she walked through it one final time before she left to pick up the kids. Their flight was coming in this afternoon and she was so excited to see them.

So much had happened since she'd seen Taylor. There was so much to tell her. So many secrets to reveal that she worried about how she would take the news.

And Alex, she'd watched his final game on Zoom and

his team had lost in the semi-finals. But it would be so good to see him. They had spoken on the phone every day and he was anxious to come to what would be their new home.

He had stayed out of trouble and she felt like her son was back. This fall he would be attending college and so would Taylor. But she wanted to spend the rest of the summer with them. To heal and show them that life had changed and moved on, and she thought for the better.

The Porsche was not big enough to take the luggage and her children. The stupid car had no back seat and she wondered why she'd made the decision to keep it. And she knew it had been an act of revenge.

A way to get even with Ryan and yet now she regretted that decision.

She might need to rethink keeping the car. Of course, on the island, they could walk just about anywhere they wanted to go.

Dylan had offered her the use of his SUV and she'd been grateful. He offered to go with her to pick them up, but she wanted some time alone with them before they learned that she was with a man, the father of their half-sister.

As she pulled up to the airport, she parked outside and stood by the car. She texted them she was out in the parking lot, anxious to see them.

And then they were walking out the door and she couldn't stop herself. She ran to her babies, throwing her arms around the both of them. Tears welled in her eyes.

They were adults, but to her, they would always remain her babies. Just like Madison.

"Taylor," she cried. "Alex."

"Mom," Taylor said, hugging her close. "Are you all right?"

"I'm fine," she said, knowing they were going to be shocked at the changes in her life.

"Mom," Alex said in his gruff manly voice. "You look different."

And she realized she was different. Relaxed and more at ease than she'd been in years.

"It's the beach," she said. "I've been spending a lot of time walking each morning and evening. And occasionally going for a dip in the ocean."

"Where did you get the car?" Taylor asked.

"It's a friend's," she said. "I didn't think we could get your luggage and you in the Porsche."

"Daddy loved that car," she said. "I'm glad you kept it."

Alex didn't say a word and neither did she. She had spoken to him before he left California and they agreed to tell her together.

But first, she wanted some time to catch up with them before she released the drama.

"Come on, guys, I can't wait for you to see what I did to the old house. Also we have dinner reservations tonight down at the Lobster Tail."

They piled in the car and Taylor pulled out her phone and started texting. She wondered what that was about.

"Mom, what made you decide to move here," she asked.

"I thought you would want to stay in Hollywood with your friends and in the house we grew up in."

This was what she feared, her daughter asking her questions because she was not ready to answer them. "I needed someplace new. And this house was paid for."

"You told me you'd never come back here," she said.

"Well, I was wrong. Wait until you see what I've done to the house. It's completely different."

Taylor sighed. "We never came here. So I have no idea what it used to look like."

"It was ugly," she said. "Really dated. My parents had not updated it in twenty years or longer. Now it's fresh. How was London?"

"So cool," she said. "If I get a chance, I'm going back over there to study again. And I met a boy there that I really like."

"Oh," she said, realizing she had not told her this before. The thought of her daughter with a man frightened her.

"Yes, but we're just keeping things light for now," she said. "I've got to finish my degree. And he does as well."

Jennifer remembered how much she had loved England. It was funny how one daughter had gone to law school and the other was studying British Literature, Jennifer's minor in college.

She pulled out into traffic and soon they were crossing the bridge to the main island.

"Wow, you can see the ocean from here," Alex said.

"Was it hard to leave California?" Taylor asked.

"Not really," Alex said. "Especially after…"

Oh no, he'd almost said something that Taylor didn't know.

"Especially after what?" Taylor said, glancing back at her brother.

"After we lost in the semi-finals," he said.

"Are you going to play baseball in college?"

"Maybe," he said.

As they drove through the town on the island, Taylor frowned. "This is really small, Mom. I can't believe you like living here. Don't you miss the fast pace of Hollywood?"

There was so much her daughter didn't understand. Maybe eventually she would, but for now, she couldn't tell her that she'd hated Hollywood, the neighborhood, and especially their neighbor.

"Not at all," she said. "We're getting close to the house. Later, maybe we can go down to the beach and swim."

"In the ocean?" Taylor said with a gasp. "But there's fish and sharks and yucky stuff in the water."

Already she was remembering how her daughter acted like a little princess and she wondered how she was going to take the news she had to deliver tonight.

"I'm all in," Alex said. "It's been forever since we swam in the ocean. The last time was that trip you took us on as a family. Dad was supposed to join us, but he never did."

"His work was so important," Taylor said.

Alex grunted, reminding Jennifer he didn't believe a word of what his father had told them every time he missed a family outing. It was Ryan's chance to be with Lustful Lily.

She turned down the street and pulled up into the

driveway. Later she'd take the SUV back to Dylan, but for now, she wanted them to see the house.

Turning the car off, Taylor stared at the house. "It seems small."

"We're not in Hollywood anymore," Alex commented.

"We could have been," she responded.

Already this was not going as planned and Jennifer's stomach started to churn. They were almost broke. Jennifer had already applied to start taking college classes and Dylan said he would help her get her degree, so she could teach.

One day, she hoped they would both be professors.

Once summer was over, she would start her classes. But she'd needed this time to get their affairs in order.

Unlocking the door, each child carried their suitcase in.

They walked in, entering the large family room with a fireplace that had seldom been used, and a large pit area where a television now hung on the wall. She'd replaced the old one with this new one she'd recently bought.

"Quaint," Taylor said.

"This is nice, Mom," Alex said.

"I've spent the last few weeks painting, replacing the appliances, the bathrooms were completely overhauled and I even bought new furniture."

Taylor turned and raised her brows. "What was wrong with our old furniture?"

"I sold it all but a few pieces when I moved here so I didn't have to hire movers."

She could see that Taylor was really confused and knew that soon she would have to tell her. The girl was going to be shocked after the elegant life they once led that had been based on lies.

"Come on, and I'll show you your rooms," she said.

They climbed the stairs into the loft area. The upper deck had a door from the loft. "You can sun outside on the deck or take the stairs to the beach from here."

She opened the first bedroom door that held the ratan bedroom set. "Taylor, this was my old room and I thought you might enjoy it."

"Thanks," she said as she went in and set her suitcase down before following Alex.

"This one is for you, Alex," she said. At a local art show, she'd found some baseball paintings she'd hung on the wall.

"You have a view of the ocean since you're in the corner bedroom," she told him. "There is a third bedroom on the other side."

That was the room she put Madison in when she visited. But they didn't need to know that just yet.

"The bathroom is through this door," she said. "Get unpacked while I fix lunch. Then we'll go down to the beach."

Alex came over and hugged her. "Mom, this house is really cool. You've done a great job."

Tears shined in her eyes. She loved this boy so very much. "Thank you. Now hurry up. I want to hear all about what you did before you left. I've missed you guys so much."

Taylor stood back and carefully stared at them. "Everything has changed. Life just feels so weird now. It's like we're no longer the same family."

It was so true in so many ways. "We're not," Jennifer said. "We'll talk more later. I want to hear about your trip to England. Unpack and then we'll talk."

How long could she put this off? How long could she delay telling Taylor the truth?

She hurried down the stairs and took out their favorite foods. She'd spent a ton of money at the grocery store yesterday, preparing for their visit.

In less than five minutes, she had a chef salad prepared for Taylor, and for Alex, she made him a meatloaf sandwich.

Upstairs, she could hear them moving around and she heard them whispering. Taylor was quizzing Alex and she just hoped her son would hold out and not tell her everything yet.

They came down for lunch, and for the next hour, she soaked up her children's stories of what they had been doing this summer. Her daughter's tales of England and her son's tales of the baseball team. Of how his coach gave him a bat with *most valuable player* inscribed on it because of how he'd grown and changed this year.

Alex had grown another foot and she could see they would need to go shopping for college. They had six weeks together before they both returned to school. Six weeks to readjust their life without their father. And to learn to accept their newest sister and even Dylan and his girls.

"Come on, let's go to the beach," she told them. They had lunch outside on the covered lower deck.

Alex was up and racing up the stairs to his room.

"Mom, I don't want to go swimming in the ocean," Taylor said.

"No problem, you can watch your brother and me from the shore," she said.

She started cleaning up the dishes.

"Why don't we have a maid anymore? Sure you would cook occasionally, but most of the time, Esmeralda did the cooking and cleaning."

Her daughter was about to get a real-life lesson.

"Let's go have fun, and tonight after dinner, we'll have a family meeting," she told Taylor. "A meeting where I'll explain my reasons for moving here. And let you know about the will."

Taylor frowned. "All right, but I'm not getting into the ocean."

"That's your choice," she said, going into her bedroom.

It was so good to have her kids here with her, but she knew there were turbulent times ahead and she wasn't certain her daughter would ever understand.

Tonight the fireworks were going to explode and she only hoped that when it was over she and Taylor were still close as mother and daughter. Alex she wasn't worried about; he knew the truth about their family. Except for Madison.

CHAPTER 21

They watched the sun slink below the horizon, casting a beautiful orange shade on the water, as they walked home from the restaurant. As much as she hated what happened to their family, she loved living here and knew she would never return to California.

Alex had a pink tinge to his skin, but by the time he went off to college, he'd sport a dark tan that would have the girls chasing him. The boy grew more handsome by the day and with his tender heart, she worried some girl would ruin him.

Sometime this summer, she was going to have to speak to him about being a responsible man. Sure they had the sex talk years ago about not sleeping with every girl who offered, but still she needed to make certain he realized how his father's infidelity had affected their family. How her own experience had affected her and Dylan and that she didn't want her children to go through what she had.

Of her two children, he was hurt the most, but still it would be good to emphasize how a responsible man acted.

"When we reach the house, I want to sit down and talk to you both about your father's will and why I moved here," she said.

Taylor's brows rose. "Why are you so serious?"

"You'll soon know," she said, not wanting to talk while they walked the beach. This was a place of enjoyment and she didn't want to taint it with what Ryan had done.

Barbara stood out on her deck and fear spiraled through Jennifer. She had met Madison. She couldn't have her say anything that would tip off the kids.

"Jennifer," she called.

"Can't stop," she answered. "I'll talk to you tomorrow."

The woman frowned and then sank back into her chair.

"Who's that?" Alex asked.

"Barbara has lived here as long as I can remember. She's a lonely little lady and we need to be kind to her," she said, thinking she really needed to invite her over after she'd told the kids they had another sister.

"She looks trashy," Taylor said. "She's wearing one of those old lady dresses."

"That you could be wearing one day," Alex told his sister.

God, she loved this kid. He understood so much more than his sister.

"Never," she said emphatically. "That's disgusting."

"One day you'll be old and it will sneak up on you," Jennifer said, wishing her daughter had more empathy like her son. But she was more like Ryan. She'd always been enamored with her father.

They reached the deck and Jennifer stepped up and unlocked the door. There was a faucet next to the deck and she rinsed her feet off and wiped them on the towel she hung there.

Alex and Taylor started in.

"Stop. Always rinse your feet off before you go in or you'll track in sand."

Taylor's brows rose, but she went over and washed her feet.

"Why don't we sit outside," Alex said.

"Not tonight," Jennifer said. She didn't want Barbara to hear what they would be talking about. Or for her to witness Taylor's reaction.

He rinsed his feet off and then the three of them walked inside.

Her daughter went over to the couch and flounced down on the furniture. Jennifer tried not to wince, knowing the girl had no idea of how to take care of things. That couch had to last a long time.

Alex came in and sank down beside her. Jennifer took the chair across from them.

She took a deep breath dreading having to tell them everything.

"Taylor after you left, I went to your father's office. The employees had not been paid in a month."

Her daughter's forehead scrunched together, a frown on her lips.

"After I spent some time going through the books, I

spoke to his head nurse and learned your father was having an affair."

Shaking her head, Taylor glared at her. "No, I don't believe you. He worked late because he had patients. Why would you believe his employees?"

This was not going to be easy.

"It seems this affair had been going on for about five years and was with Lily Jackson."

She started to laugh. "Mother, someone has been feeding you lies. He made fun of all the surgeries Ms. Jackson had. She was trash. He would never have sex with her."

"No," Alex said. "I walked in on them. Me and Kyle came home early and found them together. They were having sex in her living room. They were both naked."

Taylor stopped for a moment and stared at her brother. Jennifer could see she was starting to process the thought that her father had been cheating on her mother with Lily.

"He died in her arms," Jennifer said, unable to tell her how he really died. This was the cleaner, safer version. She didn't want her children to hate their father, but she wanted them to know the truth.

"As I went through the records, it seems your father had bought Ms. Jackson the house down the street. He'd gone through our savings, his credit cards, the money from the office, everything, taking expensive trips with Lily."

Her daughter's face appeared stunned, her mouth dropped open.

"Oh my God, we're broke?" she asked. "How can I continue to go to college? To study abroad?"

With a deep sigh, Jennifer did her best to be honest with her daughter. "We're not broke, but we're no longer rich. That's why I sold the house in Hollywood. I sold Ms. Jackson's home. Paid the employees and had a lawyer take care of everything else. Your college funds are still intact. Thank goodness, he couldn't get to that money without going through me."

Taylor covered her face with her hands. "Daddy wouldn't do this to us. There has to be insurance money, something he left for us."

"The insurance policy was canceled, and he took the cash value."

"Mom, are you going to be all right?" Alex asked. He knew how dire the situation had been. He'd been at home when she dealt with all this.

"Yes, I'm going to be fine. Between the two houses, I have enough money to live comfortably, not rich. And I'm going to go back to college this fall. I'd like to become a professor."

Right now, she felt like she was a keen professor of life.

"No, he wouldn't do this to us. He must have left something somewhere for us to find. He was a good man."

A good man as long as he kept his mistress happy and covered in jewels and furs and a big house in Hollywood. A good man who obviously didn't care about his employees or his family.

"He's your father. You should each remember him the way you want to. I know he loved you."

Taylor's eyes narrowed. "You don't love him anymore?"

How could she? The image of Dylan came to mind. No, she loved someone else.

"When a man does what your father did to his wife and children, it's very difficult for me to remember the good times. Our time together was not all bad, but I blame myself for being oblivious to the signs of his cheating. I should have checked on his spending. His trips. Blindly, I believed him until it was too late."

Stunned, Taylor sat there and shook her head. She turned to her brother. "And you knew this for how long?"

"Since about February," he said. "Why do you think my grades went down. I was so angry at him."

Thank goodness, her good son had returned once she knew of what his father had done.

"You and Mom were fighting when I came home for spring break," she said softly. "You had no idea, Mom?"

What could she say? She had stupidly not paid attention to that little voice inside her that warned her he was cheating. She'd believed he was just late dealing with his patients.

"There were signs and I ignored them. Like you, I thought he was with his patients. In surgery late at night. Not out with Lily. I never thought he would spend everything on his mistress."

Leaning into her hands, Taylor cried. "I've missed his voice so much and now I don't know how to handle his death. This summer, I thought we would be grieving for him, but you've moved on and so has Alex. I'm the only one who misses him."

Alex leaned over and took her hands from her face. "I

miss the old dad. The one who had time for us. The one who played with us when we were little. The one who made certain everything was taken care of. Not the man who spent all of his money on his mistress. Who betrayed our mom. Not the man I caught doing the act with Lily and who didn't care."

Once again, her heart warmed toward her son. Always the emphatic one who realized things would never be the same.

"Do you hate him, Mom?" Taylor asked.

"No, I said my good-byes to him before I left California. But I told him that what he had done to our family was not acceptable. And that I would never return to his grave. Never."

The door was slightly open and she could hear the surf pounding on the sand. Thunder rolled in the distance and she was surprised to hear a storm rolling in.

"What happened to Ms. Jackson?"

"Don't know and don't care," Jennifer said. Her daughter didn't need to know that information. But Alex tensed and she realized he'd been there.

"She went to jail," he said. "After she stood in the street and called Mom names, someone called the police and she refused to stop. Last I heard, she'd found a new man that was supporting her."

"That's why Kyle attacked you after the game," Taylor said and Jennifer realized she'd been watching it on television too.

"Yes," Alex said.

Taylor threw her arms around her brother. "I'm so

sorry I wasn't there. You've seen so much and I knew nothing. I feel like I've been living a lie."

"Yes," Jennifer said. "I felt the same way. So if I'm not grieving for your father, I hope you'll understand. When I learned what he'd done, it almost broke me."

"I'm so sorry, Mom," Taylor said, still hugging her brother.

A sense of relief overcame Jennifer, but she knew she had to tell them everything.

"Love you, bro," she said.

"Love you too," he said. "And yes, you missed it all. Mom selling everything, us packing up the trailer, everything."

The atmosphere no longer seemed tense and Jennifer could see that Taylor was beginning to accept the news about her father. But would she understand when her allowance for college was cut? After all, her daughter had been raised as a wealthy child.

"I'm sorry, but with two of you in college, you're going to have to live on a budget. No more just getting money whenever you need it. You'll each be given an amount to live on for a month. If you run short, you'll need to get a job."

Taylor shook her head. "Life is not going to be as easy as it was before."

"No, it's not," Jennifer said. "Soon, you'll graduate and be on your own."

"I had hoped to go to graduate school in London," Taylor said.

"Not unless you take out a loan or receive a scholarship," Jennifer said, knowing how expensive it would be for her to live in London attending school.

"It's just I met a man I really like over there," she said.

It was the first time her daughter had shown interest in a boy other than flirting or going on one or two dates. She'd been so glad her daughter had not had a serious boyfriend. But now that might have changed.

"Let's just get you through college and then we'll worry about graduate school," Jennifer said, thinking about how her daughter liked to spend money and now there was no extra. Only their college savings accounts that had to last for the next four years for her son.

"I just can't believe Daddy did this," she said.

"Would you like to see the documentation from the lawyer?" Jennifer figured she needed to let her see it with her own eyes.

"Yes," she said, glancing up. "It would help me understand."

No, it wouldn't help her to comprehend why this happened, but it would help her see how he had misused their family funds.

"I'd like to see it as well," Alex said.

"All right, in the morning, I'll find the documents and let you two look over them," she said. "I want to be as open and honest with you as I can."

How would Taylor and Alex handle the next bomb?

"There's something else you need to know. This family has had enough secrets to last a lifetime and I'm not going to keep anything from you."

Their eyes widened as they stared at their mother.

"The day your father died, I received a letter from a young woman. You see, years ago when I was seventeen, I was forced to give a baby up for adoption. She has since found me. You have an older sister that I would love for you to meet."

Stunned, her children sat there staring at her like she had grown a third head.

"Who the hell are you and what have you done with my mother," Taylor said. "Is this why you were so adamant that I not date too much and wait until I was old enough to understand the consequences before I had sex?"

"Yes," Jennifer admitted, recalling she had preached at Taylor about waiting because she didn't want her to have to go through what she had as a young woman.

"Who is the father," Alex asked her.

For the next twenty minutes, she told them the story of Madison. How her mother had forced her to give her up for adoption. How Dylan had no idea she was pregnant. How it all started right here on this beach when she was a young girl experiencing love for the first time.

They stared at her and Taylor got up and paced the room.

"In the last hour, you have destroyed my childhood. My family. My home and now even my beliefs in my mother."

Sadly, Jennifer knew she was right.

"Mom, how could you keep this a secret from us for years?" Alex asked. "Did Dad know?"

"The only persons who knew were my parents. Let me be clear, I did not want to let go of Madison, but my mother took her from my arms. I had no choice."

"Where was the father," Taylor asked.

She sighed. This would haunt her for the rest of her life.

"He didn't know. I tried to call him and write him, and he received nothing from me," she said.

"Sure," her skeptical daughter said. "You were being played, Mother."

That had been her biggest fear, but she didn't believe it was true. But the thought had crossed her young mind so many times.

"Yes, I was. We think my mother had something to do with us not getting in touch," she said. With a sigh, she knew this part would be the thing that upset them the most.

"Since I've returned here, we've become friends again. Then he learned about Madison and he was so angry with me. But we all got together and now it seems I think I'm beginning to care about him again."

"Oh, Mother," Alex said. "It's only been two months since Dad died. Don't do this."

"I agree and I told him that as well. I'm in no hurry, but sometimes you just know and, Alex, my wish for you and your girlfriend is to have the kind of love that Dylan and I have."

Alex stood. "I've heard enough. I'm going to bed."

Taylor stood as well. "My perfect family has gone to hell. I can understand you were angry with Dad, but to jump right back into a relationship with a man? A man who impregnated you and then didn't take your calls. How could you?"

"We didn't just jump right back in. It's been weeks," she

said, knowing that didn't sound long. "It's been years of us pretending we were happy with other people. This is not going to happen right away."

Alex began to climb the stairs and Taylor was right behind him.

"Next weekend, we're having a party for all of you to meet."

Her children just kept moving up the stairs like they hadn't heard her. With a sigh, she made certain the doors were locked.

After she was ready for bed, she climbed in and dialed Dylan's number.

"How did it go?"

"Not good," she said. "Taylor accepted what we told her about her Dad, but when I told them about Madison and you, they got up and went to bed."

"Give them some time. You hit them pretty hard tonight with new information," Dylan said.

"I know," she said. "I want them to accept you."

"Give it time," he said. "Believe me, my daughters are not too happy with me right now either."

She giggled.

"Where are you?" he asked.

"I'm in bed," she whispered into the phone.

"Good I am too," he said. "Want to sleep together?"

"Can't wait," she said. "But that's not happening with the kids here."

A low chuckle came from his voice.

"We could leave the phone on and snuggle together all night."

"Are you going to snore?"

"Probably," he said.

"Goodnight, Dylan," she said and laid the phone beside her pillow.

"Goodnight, Jennifer."

CHAPTER 22

A week later, Jennifer had never felt more nervous. Her children were gradually warming up to her, but it was after days of conversations where basically she asked them if they would have wanted to continue to be lied to.

All their secrets had been revealed and now she prayed that tonight's get-together would go off without a hitch and that the kids would all like one another and accept their new sister.

Somehow she feared that was not going to happen at the first meeting. As much as she loved her children, they had a burr up their butts right now because of the truth about their father and now the truth about their mother.

This summer was a big time of change for them, and she could understand why they were resisting, but it was going to happen whether they wanted it to or not. The two of them had read the lawyer's report of everything he had done and Alex had been angry. Taylor had cried, knowing her father had destroyed their rich lifestyle.

It had not been an easy couple of days, and Jennifer hoped that today, they would start the mending process, but she wasn't certain.

The doorbell rang and she jumped up and ran to it, knowing it was Madison. She had traveled from Austin and was going to spend the night. They had spoken on the phone several times and Jennifer warned her that tonight might not be the family reunion she hoped it would be.

She only hoped they would not be mean to her daughter or there could be trouble. She loved all her children and she wanted them to get along.

Opening the door, Jennifer threw her arms around Madison. "I'm so glad you're here."

Madison smiled and her eyes twinkled with happiness. "My adoptive parents would like to meet you. Maybe later this summer they'll come down with me."

"Of course," Jennifer said, thinking they were the ones her mother plotted with to take Madison away from her. For her daughter's sake, she would accept them. But it would be hard to know they chose not to give Madison the letter she wrote for her baby to read when she was older.

"Come in," she said.

When they entered the living area, both Taylor and Alex stood there staring at Madison.

"Hello," she said smiling. "I'm Madison Wilson."

"You haven't taken our last name yet," Taylor said in that snarky bitchy tone she could do so easily.

Madison shook her head. "Sorry, but I love my adoptive parents and would never hurt them by changing my name."

Jennifer glared at Taylor. Sometimes she felt like there was more of her mother in the girl than in Jennifer. Sometimes she acted just like her.

"This is my son, Alex," she said introducing her formally. "And the catty one is Taylor."

Madison held out her hand for each of them. "It's good to meet you."

"You look like our mother," Alex said, gazing at her.

"Thank you," Madison replied. "When you meet my father, you'll see that I also favor him."

Taylor turned on her heel and walked away.

"Alex, would you please carry Madison's suitcase upstairs to the room in the corner."

"Thank you," she said.

Taylor walked over and turned on the television. She turned the sound up loud as if to drown out her sister.

"Taylor, please turn that off," she said.

"I'm catching the news. Did you know that there is a tropical storm brewing out in the gulf?"

Stunned, she walked into the living room, and sure enough, they were giving a report on the remnants of a tropical storm that had moved over the Yucatan peninsula. The weather forecaster warned that with the warm waters of the Bay of Campeche there was a chance this could build into another tropical storm.

"It's nothing to worry about yet, we'll just have to watch it," she said. "Now, please turn off the television."

Her daughter acted more like a teenager than a college

student. With an obviously disgruntled sigh, she turned off the television.

"All of you come in the kitchen and help me put out the appetizers and the ingredients for our hamburgers and hot dogs."

"I am now a vegetarian," Taylor said.

This was news. Of course, she had been eating meat at the restaurant and here at home. Was this her way of trying to take the attention off of Madison? Or just making things more difficult for Jennifer.

"Fine," Jennifer said. "You can make yourself a salad."

"But I don't know how," Taylor said.

"I'll show you," Madison offered. "It'll only take a minute."

The girl almost rolled her eyes at her, but she caught her mother watching. Jennifer couldn't wait for Dylan and his girls to arrive. Maybe they could ease the tension. Or not.

She set out the paper plates, napkins, and other assorted items they needed, and just when she was going to sit down and take a breath, the doorbell rang again.

Everyone stopped and stared.

Taylor shook her head at her and Madison finished making the salad. Taylor had no kitchen skills, no cooking skills, nothing since she'd been cared for by a maid. Time for her to learn.

Jennifer went to the door and there stood Dylan with flowers in his hands. His arms were full of bouquets and she knew what the man had done.

He kissed her on the cheek and the two girls behind him stared, their eyes growing large.

"Jennifer, I'd like to introduce you to my daughters. Hannah and Sherrie," he said.

Jennifer could see that his daughters looked so much like Madison. She held out her hand and shook theirs. "It's so good to meet you. Come on in and meet the others."

Dylan walked into the living room and handed a bouquet to Madison. "For the newest member of our family."

"Thanks, Dad," she said and hugged him.

Jennifer watched as his daughters stared in bewilderment.

Then he went to Taylor and she tensed.

"I'm Dylan Anderson," he said. "You look like your mother. You must be Taylor."

"Yes, sir," she said coldly.

"I brought you flowers," he said, and for a moment, her expression flickered like she didn't know whether or not to believe he was really a bad guy.

"Thank you," she said.

"And for my own girls," he said, giving them a bouquet. "All of the women get flowers today because it's such an important day."

Running around the room, Jennifer found two big vases to put the flowers in.

Dylan approached Alex who stood in the back of the room watching everything. Her son stood with his arms crossed against his chest, his eyes narrowing.

"You must be Alex," Dylan said.

"Yes," Alex said and held out his hand for him to shake.

"Your mother talks nonstop about you kids," he said. "But she forgot to tell me how tall you are."

Alex nodded. Then he walked over and introduced himself to Hannah and Sherrie. Alex was being quite the gentleman while her daughter seemed itching to make trouble.

They had decided that before they went outside and grilled the hamburgers, they would have a short family meeting to answer questions.

Dylan picked up a wine glass and a fork and tapped on the glass.

"Attention, youngsters. Gather in the living room," he said.

They all went into the living room and sat where they could.

"I didn't know about Madison until a couple of weeks ago and Jennifer had not seen her in twenty-five years. Since the day she was born. I know this is a big surprise for all of you, but sometimes that's how life happens. And for me, it's a great surprise. Another daughter."

Glancing around the room, he took a deep breath before he went on. "Jennifer and I had not seen each other in twenty-six years and then she returned to the island. Her husband died a couple of months ago, and well, now we're just really good friends. We loved each other so much when we were kids."

Five sets of eyes gazed at him, and she feared that at any moment there was going to be a revolt.

"Our friendship, our love, for one another has been

renewed since she came back. But we both realize we have to take into consideration your feelings and emotions. We all need some time to adjust to this new life. To welcome Madison into our family. So yes, it's serious, but we're going to take it slow."

Her kids glanced at one another. "After all Taylor and Alex's father just passed away a couple of months ago and we need to respect his memory."

Taylor's brows rose and she glanced at her brother.

"Anyone have any questions?"

"Yes," Hannah said, glancing at her sister. "Did Madison bring you guys back together?"

Jennifer smiled at Madison who seemed to be standing off to the side alone.

"Yes, she did," Dylan said, smiling at Jennifer. "When I learned about her, I was very upset with Jennifer, but Madison helped me to realize that Jennifer would have found me if she could have and told me about the pregnancy."

"Wow," Taylor said out loud. "How young were you when you got my mother pregnant?"

"I was seventeen," Dylan said. "And then one day she just disappeared off the island. No matter how many times I called her or wrote her letters, she never answered. And now the child we created has brought us back together."

Jennifer watched the expressions on their children's faces and knew they were not out of the woods yet. That there was still animosity between them, even though they had just met.

"Any other questions?"

"Are the two of you sleeping together," Alex asked.

A blush spread across her cheeks and she was shocked that her son would ask that question. But then she had to think about what his father had done.

"No, we're not. We're waiting," Dylan responded.

Giggles spread through the room and she noticed how Madison was not included. What could she do to make them accept her?

"If no one else has any questions, let's cook the hamburgers and hot dogs," Jennifer said standing.

The kids began to talk amongst themselves.

"Can I help you?" Madison asked.

"Please," Jennifer responded as they went outside onto the sandy part of the beach and Dylan lit the grill. Amazed that Taylor had not offered, she noted her son and daughter were sitting off to the side talking between themselves.

Soon they were all outside sitting around the table, eating hot dogs and hamburgers, and talking, though the words sometimes sounded stilted.

"Where do you go to school, Madison," Alex asked.

"I'm in law school at the University of Texas in Austin," she said.

Talk of college began to spread around the table and Dylan placed his hand on her leg beneath the table. He winked at her and she knew he believed that everything was going fine, but she was still not certain.

Hostility seemed to be hovering just beneath the surface and she felt that at any moment, something was going to happen.

Suddenly Taylor appeared in the doorway with the chocolate cake she'd made earlier in the day. She walked to the table and then a sly grin appeared as she fell forward and smashed the cake on Madison's head.

Stunned, Jennifer stared at her and saw the devilment in her eyes.

Madison stood, wiped the cake out of her hair, and then she turned and threw it at Taylor. "You did that on purpose."

Alex took exception and he picked up his soft drink and threw it on Madison. Then Dylan's two girls threw their beverages on Alex.

With disbelief, Jennifer and Dylan watched as their families battled one another. "Madison is our sister. You don't mistreat her," Hannah said, picking up a chunk of the cake and throwing it at Taylor.

Alex grabbed her hand and she turned what she had left of the cake on him, smearing it across his face.

Sherrie reached for a glass of soda and tossed it on Taylor. "Have some Coke to go with your chocolate cake. You're a real snooty little bitch."

"She's not a part of our family," Taylor cried. "She's just a poor kid who was given up by two teenagers."

Dylan made to stand and Jennifer laid her hand on his arm. Maybe they should get all their issues out in the open like this. Then she and Dylan would step in and chastise them all.

Alex growled at his sister. "Why do you always have to be so mean. We were lucky to get to live with our parents. She didn't. Do you ever consider anyone else's feelings?"

There was her caring son again and she loved that he always managed to think of others. But her daughter was not the same.

Madison gave him a thumbs up and he grinned at her.

The kids suddenly turned on Taylor.

"Why did you have to ruin our evening," Sherrie said. "Madison is our sister and we wanted to get to know her."

Taylor kind of took a step back. Whatever happened she deserved what the kids said to her.

"Did you ever think that we were just as scared of meeting her as you were? Why did you have to act up? Now look at all of us, we're covered in cake and you're still being a bitch," Hannah said.

They were all yelling at one another and Madison suddenly put her fingers to her lips and whistled. It grew silent.

"I didn't expect to be accepted right away. I'm the oddball that none of you knew about until a few days ago. But I'm still a human being with feelings. You don't know what it's like not to know who your family is. What they look like. What your history is. You have no access to medical information. To know where you come from, who your grandparents, aunts, and uncles are. I didn't have any of that. Growing up, I stared into strangers' faces to see if they resembled me. But now I have Mom and Dad. Now I have you, whether you want me or not."

With that, she walked into the house.

Jennifer stood. "I'm ashamed of how you all acted tonight. Especially you, Taylor. That could have been you, but by the grace of God, it wasn't. Now I expect this patio to be scrubbed clean of any mess. Get started. Dylan and I have to console Madison."

Dylan's chair scraped against the concrete and they walked into the house.

"Damn, darling, you're good."

She smiled at him. "Though it doesn't look like it, I think we made some progress tonight. Did you see how your girls were defending Madison? I'm sure there will be more battles, but the first skirmish is now history."

Shaking his head, Dylan and she climbed the stairs to Madison's room.

When they knocked on the door, she opened it with a smile. "How did I do?"

Laughing, Jennifer hugged her even though she was sticky with cake. "I think you're going to make a fine lawyer."

"You did that on purpose?" Dylan asked.

"I didn't start it, but when I saw where it was going, I tried to turn the tide in my direction," she said. "I'm practicing and I think I won this round."

Running his hand through his hair, Dylan stared at their daughter. "You're good. But are you all right?"

"I'm fine," she said. "And as soon as they finish cleaning, I expect they will be coming up here to apologize. This will make us closer in the long run."

Jennifer turned and smiled at Dylan. "Our daughter is very smart."

"Damn straight," he said. "Let's go clean the kitchen and see if they come to apologize."

First, Alex went up the stairs and knocked on her door,

then the others one by one. Taylor was the last one, but even she eventually went upstairs to see Madison.

Later that evening, Dylan called Jennifer on the phone.

"Good night, Jennifer," he said. "I think our family is on its way to coming together."

She smiled.

"Next time we get together, I'm not going to bake a cake," she said. "Or a pie. Nothing that they can throw at one another."

"Kids are resourceful. I'm just glad it was a cake and not something dangerous."

"Me too," she said, wondering what tomorrow would bring. "I just hope they don't try to tear us apart."

"Not happening," he said.

But she feared what they could do to separate the two of them.

CHAPTER 23

The gulf had been rough the last couple of days and they were starting to get bands of rain from the tropical storm they hoped and prayed would take a turn and head back into the gulf or in a different direction.

Every day, they tried to do something with their children as a group, hoping they would grow closer. Hoping they would accept Madison. And every day, she saw a little progress.

The clouds were looming over the sea and she knew they would soon be forced to go inside until the rain subsided. A storm brewing in the gulf was unnerving, but not enough to make her move inland. She loved her little beach house and didn't plan on moving again.

Today, she and Dylan were lying on the beach watching their grown children play beach volleyball with occasional dips in the rough sea.

"Something is going on," Dylan said. "Sherrie and Alex

are laughing and giggling and I don't like what I see. They're doing that dance of courtship."

"They're kids. We'll just have to keep an eye on them, but they both leave for college in three weeks. No time for a summer fling."

"Would that have stopped us?" Dylan asked.

With a sigh, she knew he was right. "But things were different then. You don't hear of kids having wet T-shirt parties or getting drunk or even having sex on the beach."

He glanced at her and shook his head. "We don't hear about it because we're the parents. They probably do. Nothing has changed between the sexes. It's still that attraction that draws us to someone special."

Right now, she just wanted her son and daughter to accept Madison and even Hannah and Sherrie. She wasn't worried about them having sex on the beach unlike her and Dylan at that age.

"You worry more than I do," she said.

"I'm very protective of my daughters. Some guy is not going to take them behind a sand dune and get them pregnant," he said.

She didn't like his tone. "But it was okay for you to?"

"No, if we had not had that spiked punch, we would not have gone so far that night."

"I have fond memories of that night," she said.

"I feel guilt," he said. "Especially after learning about Madison. What we did put you through so much and I should have been there."

The man had no idea how she'd felt during those months of carrying his child.

"When I was pregnant, I had so many doubts about you. I thought that maybe you just used me. I was the summer fling, and now that I was pregnant, you wanted nothing to do with me. Especially when I didn't hear from you."

With a sigh, he reached out and grabbed her hand. "Not at all. It never crossed my mind that you were pregnant, though I was pretty stupid for not considering it. We were careful. We didn't let things go too far until we had a little alcohol in us. And yet, look at our daughter, she's smart and beautiful, and frankly, I wish we had half a dozen more just like her."

So did Jennifer, but she was past the baby-making stage. Right now, she'd just settle for them all to get along.

"Where are Sherrie and Alex?" she asked, glancing around the beach. They were gone. "Are they in the water?"

"No," he said, rising from his beach chair.

She glanced at her daughter Taylor. "Where is Alex?"

Taylor shrugged. "I don't know. His team won at volleyball, so we decided to take a break. Besides, the clouds are rolling in. Looks like it's going to storm again."

At that moment the wind picked up.

"Let's pack up," Dylan called out. "Looks like another rain band is rolling in."

Madison and Hannah were in the water. Thunder boomed in the distance.

"Everyone out," he called. "It's time to go home."

Taylor grabbed her towel and beach bag, and slowly the girls made it out of the water. They all started to pack up. But there was no sign of Sherrie and Alex.

"Head to the house and I'll look for the kids," he said, a worried look on his face.

Something was going on. She knew her son. She knew he would not do anything inappropriate, but he was a young boy who liked girls and had never had a serious relationship.

Hormonal teens often got into trouble. She had gotten into trouble.

"No, I'm going to stay with you," she said. "Alex wouldn't just wander away like this."

She wasn't leaving until she found him.

"Girls, head to the house. As soon as we find Alex and Sherrie, we'll meet you there."

She gave Taylor her keys and the three girls left carrying most of their stuff.

Lightning flashed across the sky and she began to get scared.

"Alex," she called. The wind picked up and they walked toward the sand dunes. No, they wouldn't. No.

They knew their history. They knew the consequences. It was daylight and they were not filled with alcohol.

Stepping behind several dunes, she saw them. Alex had Sherrie down on the ground and he covered her body with his, lying directly on top of her. His mouth on hers, his hand…

"Alex," she yelled.

The two came apart and the top of Sherrie's bathing suit was down.

"What the hell," Dylan said and grabbed Alex and yanked him up.

"Daddy," she said. "Stop."

Dylan's fist pulled back and Jennifer grabbed his hand. He couldn't punch her son. She would not let him.

"Don't ever touch my daughter again, do you understand me?"

He reared back to try to hit him and Jennifer laid her hand on his shoulder. "Stop. Don't you dare, hit my son."

Dylan's face was red and she knew how upset he was. And she was upset as well. But violence would not solve the problem and somehow she got the feeling this was staged.

"Alex, get to the house now."

"Mom," he said ready to defend her from Dylan. "I'm not leaving without you."

"This is not right," Dylan said. "It's disrespectful to my daughter."

"Just like you were disrespectful to my mother," Alex said suddenly looming large over Dylan. "You got her pregnant and never married her. You're worse than my father."

She could see Dylan was struggling to say something. But there was something else she detected. Sherrie was grinning and she wondered if the kids had planned this little skirmish.

Before she could confront them, the clouds opened up, pouring rain on them. Everyone scrambled.

She glared at Sherrie whose smile suddenly faded. If they were this determined to keep them apart, did she still want to be with Dylan? How could they overcome this kind of intentional prank to come between her and Dylan?

And he'd almost punched her son.

They took off running to get out of the weather, but she hung back. Things had gotten out of hand. They had gone too far and she couldn't deal with this now. The last week, it had been one prank after another, but this one was by far the worst.

Suddenly it felt like the world was crashing in on her and she needed to take a step back and reconsider. She'd just gotten out of one loveless marriage; was she really ready to jump into another relationship?

When they reached the house, it was still pouring rain and the girls were standing on the covered deck watching them.

"Let's go," Dylan said and she realized he had not apologized to Alex or even turned to her and acknowledged that he'd made a mistake.

"Girls, in the car, we're going home," he said and he hurried his kids through the house and into his car.

At the last second, he turned to her but said nothing. She went inside, shut the door, and locked it.

"You won," she said to her children.

The two of them stood there speechless as she went into her room and crawled into the shower. She needed time and space.

While part of her thought they had created this scene to come between them, she realized just how well their plan had worked. Dylan left without saying good-bye or apologizing. Alex got his say in and let Dylan know his feelings for how he'd treated her years ago.

If they could do this to them, did they really have as good of a foundation as she'd believed?

In the shower, she cried away the frustration of the day. Maybe they were not meant to be together. Maybe her mother had been right and he was not the man for her.

When she finally climbed out of the shower, she dressed and pulled out her phone. Three missed calls from Dylan.

She needed some space. She needed time to reflect if this was really going to work with their children plotting against them. A divorced mother told her once that the kids always wanted the parents to get back together. Could Sherrie and Hannah want their parents to get back together and would they do anything to tear Dylan and Jennifer apart?

When she walked out of the bedroom, she found her children in front of the television.

They were watching the local station. "All residents are urged to prepare for Hurricane Edward, and if you live on the island, it's recommended that you evacuate. Right now, the winds are a category one, but that could change by morning."

Great! The tropical storm was now a hurricane and they were being urged to leave.

"Mom, are we going to evacuate?"

"It's only a category one," she said. "I don't know. I really don't want to go."

She had just finished the house and now a storm was headed their way. She didn't want to deal with the drama of a hurricane. She was dealing with the drama of a mutiny. Besides, how would she get four adults into the Porsche?

Her phone rang again and it was Dylan. She turned it off.

The rain had stopped and yet the sea was crashing into the shore like she'd never heard it before.

The house had hurricane shutters and with the touch of a button, she could have the windows covered. Even the patio doors would be sealed tight against the waves and the wind. Unless the house crumbled beneath the onslaught of the wind and water, they should be safe.

Still, she had best prepare in case they had to leave. The meteorologist showed where the storm was and the predicted path. It seemed to be heading right toward them.

"Damn," she said. "Okay, listen up. Everyone pack a bag of what you can't live without. Taylor that does not mean everything you own. It must all fit into the Porsche because that's all I have to drive."

"I've got my car," Madison said. "We could leave in it."

Her Volkswagen wasn't much bigger than the Porsche.

"You can take your car and Alex can ride with you. Taylor and I will take the Porsche. Be prepared. We may have to leave at a moment's notice."

The local newscaster came on and showed the evacuation routes off the island – one by car and one by boat. And sadly, the boat would stop operating in the morning. The first squalls could reach them at dawn. They were telling everyone to leave now.

She felt paralyzed. She didn't want to abandon her home. And yet she had these three beautiful children with her that she felt responsible for.

How could she risk their lives? Because once the storm started, they would not be leaving the island. The wind would blow them off the bridge and she refused to take that chance.

And what about Dylan and his girls?

Right now, she had to focus on getting everything ready to go. The power would go out, so she would need to clean the fridge. They could be without power for days. She packed a bag, cleaned out the safe, packed the insurance papers, and then went in search of the photos.

Grabbing a plastic tub, she put the photos in the container and also her jewelry and some other things she wanted to save.

She was going through the house room by room when the doorbell rang.

Immediately, she knew it was Dylan.

Damn.

This couldn't be avoided.

She opened the door and then turned to go back to what she was doing. "I'm kind of busy right now."

"Stop," he said. "We need to talk."

"No, I'm busy," she said. "Go away. I don't want to talk."

His girls followed him in and they looked sheepish.

"Stay away from my son," she said, glaring at Sherrie.

"That's what we need to talk about," Dylan said. "It was a setup."

She stopped. They were in the family room.

"Everyone, gather round," Dylan said.

"I can't do this," she said. "You kids were successful.

Dylan and I are done. I hope you're all happy. I give up, you win."

Dylan's face fell and she could see he was sad. "Just listen, Jennifer, before you make any decisions."

"Alex, first I owe you an apology. I should never have tried to hit you. But you and Sherrie did this to end our relationship. You wanted to do what your mother and I had done behind the sand dunes, and get caught, knowing you could make me look really bad and break us up. And damn it, I reacted exactly like you wanted me to."

Jennifer stared at her son and knew that Dylan was right. Plus, she'd caught Sherrie grinning when her father and Alex got into a fight, though she'd been crying for her daddy to stop.

"Here's the thing," Dylan said. "I love Jennifer and I don't want this to end because our bratty children can't accept that we've found love with someone besides who they want. I'm never getting back with your mother, Sherrie. Never. Don't you want me to be happy?"

"Yes," she said in a tearful whisper.

"Then why are you being so selfish? And, Alex, I would have married your mother in a heartbeat if I'd known she was pregnant. I can't change the past. We're waiting because your mother needs more time. We're not rushing into marriage. Do you want your mother to be happy?"

"Yes, sir," he said with a heavy sigh. "But I saw how my father treated her and I'm not going to accept any man who disrespects her. You disrespected her once already."

He was right, but it had not been intentional.

"I give you my word that I will never disrespect your mother ever again."

There was silence in the room and Jennifer didn't know how she felt at this moment. Today seemed to have been the breaking point for her.

"Does anyone else have any objections to the two of us being together?"

"I do," Jennifer said. "If your children don't want me and my children don't want you, I think we should give up. I can't battle them any longer. I'm done."

She got up and went into the kitchen and started to throw out food that would not last.

First, Hannah came into the kitchen. "I'm sorry for being so difficult," she said. "You make my father happy. I haven't seen him this happy in years and that scared me. I was afraid you would take him away from me."

Jennifer glanced up. "He's your father. I would never do that. All I wanted was for you girls to accept me. For my children to accept that we could be one big happy family. But that's obviously an unrealistic dream. I knew it would be hard, but I've had enough strife and stress in my life this year and I can't take anymore."

Hannah's eyes filled with tears. "I'm sorry."

Jennifer renewed her energy on the refrigerator.

Next came Sherrie. "I want to apologize," she said. "We wanted to break up the two of you, because…you're not our mother."

"And I never will be," Jennifer said, her irritation evident. "But you endangered my son. If you had accepted me, I would have treated you like one of my own children.

Protecting you, loving you, and wanting your happiness. But instead you made your father almost punch my son. Someday you'll understand how it feels when someone wants to hurt your child. And believe me, I'm just as mad at him as I am at you."

Sherrie started crying and while part of Jennifer felt bad, she had no urge to make her feel better. She was pissed, royally pissed at them all. Including her own children.

Taylor walked through the door and came over and hugged her.

"Did you have a part in this?"

"I knew about it," she said. "I went along with it."

"Then you're just as bad as the rest of them. Why is it my children and Dylan's children don't think we deserve happiness? Do you think I was happy with your father? Let me tell you about him. He was screwing the neighbor down the street and had been for *five* years. They were having sex when he had his heart attack. And now my children think they're protecting me from finding happiness with a man I've loved for years. I always promised that I would never interfere when you found the one you wanted to marry, well, maybe I should. Maybe I should try to break you up."

Taylor took a step back, her eyes wide, her face stunned.

"Mom," she said with a gasp, "I've never seen you this way before."

"I'm tired of life trying to screw me over," she said. "And it really hurts when my children are involved."

"I'm sorry, Mom. I should have told you," she said.

For the first time in her life, Jennifer was so angry at her family that she wanted to run, not walk, away from them.

"You should have told them not to do it and then you should have told me," she said. "Get out of the kitchen."

At this point, cleaning the refrigerator was more of an exercise in just tossing out all the rotten stuff in her life. She wanted it gone. All of it.

Next came Alex. "Mom, I'm sorry. But he did you wrong once and I couldn't let him do what Dad had done to you."

This one was tougher. And yet he'd been just as wrong as Sherrie and Hannah and even Taylor.

"Alex, your father did me really dirty, but Dylan did not. We were two young kids who the adults kept apart. For the first time in my life, I felt really happy, and Dylan was the man who had made me that way. But then you and Sherrie put a real wedge in our relationship. How can I love a man who almost punched my son?"

"That's what we wanted to happen," he said, his voice almost a whisper. "Because I knew that would be the final straw for you. I thought I was protecting you from getting hurt again."

Astonished, she looked up at her son. For the first time in months, she was truly angry at him.

"Damn you, Alex," she said. "You've put me in a bad place. For the first time in years, I was happy and you and Sherrie managed to ruin that happiness. Is that what you wanted?"

"I'm sorry, Mom," he said. "We thought we were protecting our parents."

"Do you want me to protect you when you fall in love? Do you want me to break up you and your girlfriend? Think about it from my perspective for a change. That's what my mother did to me. She separated me from Dylan just like you and Sherrie are trying to do."

His face blanched. "I'm sorry, Mom. I won't interfere again."

"Leave me be," she said. "I need some time."

Just then Dylan walked into the kitchen. "Sorry, but you can't have time. They just ordered a mandatory evacuation of the island. Grab whatever you want, we're leaving."

Tears filled her eyes. "No, I'm not going. Take the kids. I'm staying."

The thought of leaving with Dylan and his girls was more than she could take right now. She had to have time alone to decide what she could handle. And marrying Dylan didn't seem to be what she could do.

"Jennifer, I'm not going to leave you."

The kids came running into the kitchen.

"Mom, we all have to leave. It's not safe," Madison said.

"I'm not going if you're not going," Hannah said. "We want you with us."

Sherrie teared up. "Please, Jennifer. If something happened to you, we'd feel awful."

"None of us are leaving if you don't go," Alex said.

"None of us," Taylor warned.

She stared at the young faces in front of her. She had to protect them. She had to go.

"All right, but I'm warning you, I'm on edge. You guys have pushed me to the end and one little thing and I'm going to dig my heels in and stay."

She glared at Dylan. "And you—don't you ever think about hitting one of my kids again."

CHAPTER 24

The children began to load up all the backpacks and boxes she'd hurriedly packed. Watching them, she gazed around the house she'd recently renovated and fallen in love with. What would she do if the hurricane destroyed the house?

Right now, she couldn't even contemplate that happening. It would send her over the brink and she was precariously close as it was.

Once everything was loaded, they walked the house, shutting the hurricane shutters and even putting the new furniture up on the second floor where they covered it with plastic. Maybe it was an exercise in futility, but it couldn't hurt.

When they were ready to leave, she looked around the house one last time and sadness overwhelmed her. The Hollywood home she'd left gladly, but this one she didn't want to leave.

It was then she saw they had forgotten the clock.

"Alex, grab the clock," she said. "That was your great-grandfather's."

He picked it up from the sides and the bottom fell to the floor. Letters spilled out. He picked them up and then he glanced at her with the oddest expression on his face. "They're letters from you to Dylan."

"What?"

Dylan and she hurried to his side and picked up the remaining letters. There were letters from her to Dylan and letters he'd written her. Even the letter from her to the baby. Her mother had kept them all.

"Oh my God," she said. "She never mailed them, just like I thought."

"But she saved them."

"Look, here's one addressed to you," he said. "And a letter to my baby girl."

Just then a big gust of wind hit the house.

"We've got to go," he said. "We'll read them when we get to the house my friend has. They're in Europe and he has a home on the mainland where we can stay."

Gazing at the letters brought back so many memories of her feelings that she stood there mesmerized.

Finally, Dylan took her by the arm. "Are you taking the Porsche?"

"No," she said. "It doesn't do well in high water. We'll ride with you, though Madison and Alex are going to take her car."

"Let's go, we'll follow them in case they run into trouble."

Jennifer stuffed the letters into her purse, took one last look at the house she loved, and walked out the door.

"We've got to get Barbara," she cried.

"You're right," Dylan said.

She called the elder. "Are you ready to leave?"

"I'm staying," she said.

"No, you're going with us. We'll be at your house in five minutes. Pack a small suitcase."

"Are you certain this is necessary?"

"Your house is lower than mine. It's absolutely necessary," Jennifer said. "We're on our way."

When they pulled up in front of her home, Jennifer ran to the door and helped the woman to the car. Dylan ran up and grabbed the few boxes of things she'd taken.

"Where are your storm shutters," he said. "Why aren't they down?"

"Don't have them. They're too expensive," she told him as they pulled away from the house.

The rain was coming down in sheets. Dylan and his girls had already packed up their house and closed it up with the hurricane shutters.

As they drove toward the ferry, the road covered with deep water. So they turned toward the bridge that connected the mainland and the island.

In horror, she watched Madison's Volkswagen blow sideways in the wind on the bridge.

Terror seized Jennifer as she watched the baby she loved battle the wind.

"No," Hannah cried. "Our brother and sister are in that car."

If Jennifer had not been so frightened, she would have been thrilled at Hannah's words of acceptance. But right now she was terrified.

"She's all right," Dylan said. "She straightened it up. But I'll be glad when we get on the mainland."

"This is more dangerous than staying at home," Barbara told them from the back seat.

Ten minutes later, they all sighed with relief when the little yellow bug crossed onto the main road. Madison pulled to the side and Dylan passed her to guide them to his friend's house.

"Watch and make certain she's behind us," Jennifer said to the girls in the back seat.

Thirty minutes later, they pulled up in front of a big home.

"Stay here until I get the house open," he said.

"Wow, this is a fancy place," Barbara said.

The rain continued to come down. Soon there were lights on in the house and he even opened the garage door. The spacious three-car garage had room for both vehicles.

Dylan pulled the SUV in and Madison followed him.

Everyone piled out of the car.

"We were so scared you were going over the side of the bridge," Sherrie said, running to Madison.

Alex shook his head. "That was pretty scary. But Madison held on tight and we made it, obviously."

Thunder rumbled and Jennifer gave Madison and Alex a hug. "Let's get in the house."

Barbara walked into the place and glanced around. "Are

you sure we're supposed to be here? This is an awful fancy place. I'm too old to go to jail."

Dylan walked past her and carried backpacks in.

"My friend is in Europe and he said we could stay," Dylan told her.

"He must have money," she said. "A shit ton of money."

"And he's glad we're here to put the hurricane shutters down."

Once inside, Dylan went to every window and pushed the button for the window barriers to cover them. It made the house feel eerie and dark.

"George told me there is a supply of LED candles and flashlights in the utility room. He recommended that we all sleep in the main room. There are sleeping bags in the garage. Oh, and we need to draw some water in case we lose the water supply."

For the next thirty minutes, they set up their camping area and Jennifer even made them snacks to eat.

Barbara sat in a recliner and watched them all running around.

"Damn, this is like a big ol' sleepover," she said.

Finally when everything was prepared, they gathered together.

"Before we lose power, why don't you read the letters," Dylan said.

"No," she said. "I'll read mine to you and you read yours to me."

A grin spread across his face.

They were all gathered together and Jennifer picked up her letter.

Dearest Dylan,

On Friday morning, my parents woke me up early and whisked me back to Dallas. I wanted to tell you good-bye, but my mother wouldn't allow it. Now we're back at home and when I try to call you, you don't answer the phone.

There's something you need to know. That night on the beach when the condom broke, I became pregnant. Yes, I'm expecting our child and I'm afraid. My parents want me to give the baby up for adoption, but this is a part of us. Our child. Please call me so we can decide what to do.

I'm so worried that I haven't heard from you.

Love,

Jennifer

"What the hell are you reading?" Barbara asked.

"It's letters that Jennifer and I wrote to each other years ago," Dylan told her.

All the emotions from that time came rushing back like high tide. She remembered being filled with terror.

Dear Jennifer,

Where are you? What happened? You won't answer my phone calls, so I'm trying to reach you by letter. I went to your house, but you weren't there.

Did I make you mad? Why aren't you returning my calls?

You know I love you and I don't understand what's going on. We had three more weeks before the summer ended. Please call me.

Love,

Dylan

They read each other's letters, each one sounding more

and more desperate. Until the last one from Jennifer had them all crying.

Dylan,

Yesterday, I delivered our baby girl. Oh, how I wanted you to come and rescue us. To marry me and raise this child we created. But I've heard nothing from you. Nothing.

Today, Mother took the child from me and told me there was a good family that is going to raise her. I begged and pleaded with her not to take my baby, but she refused to hear me. I refused to sign the adoption papers, but I think she must have forged my signature.

Why have you not answered my letters? Do you not care about our daughter? Do you no longer love me? Right now, I hate you for what you've put me through. For the loss of our child.

I'm going to get her back and then I'm going to find you and show you what you're missing.

Jennifer

There was silence in the room and all of the girls were crying.

"Last letter," Jennifer said quietly. "And it's from my mother."

Dearest Jennifer,

I know you hate me and I understand why. But I wanted to give you the best possible life and having a child out of wedlock at your age would not have been easy. What you don't know is that I cried for weeks after we gave up the baby. I watched you walk around with a haunted look in your eyes and realized the pain you were in. And then when you left for college, I knew I had lost my daughter forever.

Oh, you came back to visit twice a year, but you never were the young woman who loved me before. You never forgave me for what I'd done.

And I was wrong.

I disregarded Dylan's phone calls. I hid his letters. I never mailed your letters to him because I thought I was doing what was right. But all my actions did was drive you farther away from me.

And I lied to you about the parents wanting you to see their baby. They wanted a closed adoption with you having no access to the child.

Sometimes as a parent you think you're protecting and helping your child when all you're doing is interfering and hurting them.

When you find this letter, I'm certain I will be long gone from this world. All I can say is that I'm sorry. I interfered with the best of intentions and it cost me the one thing I loved most in this world. You.

Love,

Mom

Tears ran down her cheeks and Dylan pulled her into his arms and held her.

"Now we know," he said. "God, I would have come and rescued you and Madison. I would have married you and loved you, just like I do now. Your mother cheated us from a life we could have had."

They both cried for the life they lost.

One by one, their children came to them and wrapped their arms around them.

"We'll be together now," Madison said softly.

"Always," Sherrie said. "You two were meant to be together. That's so very obvious."

"No more fighting," Taylor said against her mother's shirt. "We're a family."

"I think we're going to need a bigger house," Alex said.

Barbara blew her nose real loud and joined them in their group hug. "I'm not family, but damn, that was heart wrenching. Why do I always have the best time with you kids?"

They pulled her into their fold.

Jennifer stared into Dylan's eyes and saw the shimmering tears.

"I love you, Jennifer, and when you're ready, please marry me," Dylan said. "And make us one big happy family."

Her heart swelled with love, and though they weren't on the island, she felt like she'd come home. All the trials of the last few months had brought her to this moment and she was glad.

"Yes," she said. "A thousand times yes."

The kids all squeezed them and jumped up and down with joy.

"We can plan the wedding," Taylor said laughing.

"On the beach," Jennifer said, "where we met."

"Where we fell in love as young kids," Dylan said.

"Where our family came back together," Madison said.

"I love you all," Hannah said. "But especially Jennifer for making my dad so happy and bringing us all together."

"Yes," the children cried.

"My heart has always been yours," Dylan said. "I'll be by your side through the rest of my days, happily loving you."

With her heart overflowing with love, Jennifer felt like she'd come full circle. Yes, it was way too early for her to remarry, but this man she'd loved for years.

Just then a powerful blast of wind shook the house and the power sputtered and died. The reality of what they were facing made her lean into Dylan more.

Life was too short not to spend it with those you loved. At the first opportunity, she would marry him.

"Time to hunker down," Dylan said. "We have a hurricane to live through."

"And a wedding to plan," Jennifer said softly.

CHAPTER 25

The sun shone brightly through the window, the sound of the surf a lull that called to her each day.

Today was her wedding day. It had been three weeks since the hurricane. Two days before the children all packed up and headed back to school. They had spent every day working on the cleanup from the hurricane and planning the wedding. Every child had a part in the ceremony.

The hurricane had turned easterly and come in farther up from their beach. Thank God it had, but the destruction had still been major on the island. The Lobster Tail had been flattened, but they promised to rebuild even stronger.

The first hurricane to hit in almost a hundred years – downed palm trees, roofs torn off homes, water damage, and even road destruction. With the storm being a category three, they were lucky everything was still standing.

The post office was still there, though it needed a new

roof. The grocery store had reopened, but the power had been out long enough that they gave away their frozen food to anyone on the island.

The power had been the worst thing. With downed lines everywhere, the electricity had been turned off until everything could be restored.

Barbara's home was damaged because she did not have hurricane shutters. The repairmen were replacing the broken glass and fixing the water damage she received along with new hurricane shutters, new paint, and carpet.

The older woman was so excited about the updates they were doing on her beach house. But she refused to leave the place and was back living amongst the construction.

Jennifer's home needed a new roof. The old one was still on, but it leaked and she ran around putting buckets everywhere to minimize the water damage. She felt fortunate.

Dylan's house had suffered some water damage, but only one side of the house needed repairs. The rest of the house was fine.

During the hurricane, they played games in the glow of the candles while listening to the wind howl outside and objects hit the house. Until, one by one, the children fell asleep. And yet she and Dylan had sat and talked and talked and talked until morning arrived with less wind, but still squalls of rain.

It was a night filled with promises of their life together, talk of commitment to one another, and their feelings about the past.

And yet all night, there had been a sense of safety and

serenity that kept Jennifer from panicking or even worrying about their safety. All the people she loved were together in one spot and she knew they were safe.

Their love was like a fortress and nothing could hurt them now. And the children might try to separate them, but they would never let that happen.

They spent three nights at the house before they were allowed back on the island. Since then, they had managed to start the repairs needed and plan a wedding. Dylan and the girls had moved to a hotel, though she had told them they could stay with her.

Sadly, the sand dune where Madison had been conceived was no more. The wind and the waves had blown it away. Maybe it was for the best.

And yet she and the baby she'd been forced to give up grew closer every day. Remembering the day she received that letter, her heart tightened. What a wonderful surprise. One she would be forever thankful for. A letter that she had saved along with all the others, including the one she wanted given to Madison when she was old enough to understand.

A knock sounded on her bedroom door. "Mom, are you ready?"

It was Alex. Her all-grownup son was walking her down the makeshift aisle. The dress she'd chosen was shin-length and white. She wore no shoes and the girls had each chosen a dress they liked.

There were flowers in her hair on an ornate headband. No veil. Nothing fancy.

It was not a formal wedding by any means, and yet,

she'd loved the excitement the children had helping to plan the event. This was their family joining celebration and it brought them all even closer.

She opened the door and smiled at this boy she loved with all her heart.

"The girls have all walked down and everyone is waiting on you."

Without thinking, she reached up and cupped his cheek. "You are going to be a good man, Alex. A man not like your father, but a man who will cherish his family. I'm looking forward to seeing what you do with your life."

"Mom," he said. "Now come on or Dylan's going to think I'm trying to talk you out of this."

She laughed. "No, son. No one could keep me from that man. He's my life, my destiny."

Taking her son's arm, they walked through the house and out into the bright sunshine. Dylan stood waiting for her near the area of the beach where they had first fallen in love. Their girls were all lined up. Madison and Alex would stand up with them and be their witnesses, but the other girls were bridesmaids.

As they walked through the sand toward the man she loved, she knew this was what she'd been waiting for her entire life.

When they reached the beach, the preacher glanced over them.

"Who gives away this woman," the preacher asked.

The children all spoke at once, "We do."

The crowd of friends all laughed.

Though they were older, she and Dylan were wiser, and

she knew they would spend the rest of their days living on this wonderful island that she had never wanted to return to because of all the pain she'd felt that summer.

But now, the secrets of a summer place were all revealed. Now she had more than she'd ever dreamed possible. Now nothing, not children, a storm, or even death could keep them apart. They would always be one.

* * *

Look for Secrets of a Runaway Bride Crystal's story—
February 2023

AUTHOR'S NOTE

Adoption can be a wonderful thing. In our family, we have four adopted children and each one has their own story. My sister, Debra was an adopted child that we loved and wanted very much. It was difficult for her to accept how much we wanted her and she longed to find her birth mother, father, and half-brother. We searched for them and she even went before a judge and asked him to open the adoption documents.

He refused.

In the end, her life became a tragedy. At the age of fifty-two, she suffered a brain aneurysm and died. I've often wondered if this was an inherited medical condition, but we will never know because we don't know her family background.

To her birth parents, I wish that you would have met with her and answered her questions. I think she would have been a much happier person. That gaping hole in her personality would have been filled with the knowledge that

AUTHOR'S NOTE

you could have provided. She would know who she looks like, who she takes after, and could have accepted you decision.

This story is my version of what I would have liked to see my sister's life become. Not the life she lived. And think about it, what if you didn't know anything about your birth parents. What they looked like, their medical conditions, their history, etc. It would be a gaping hole in your life.

We do know that her mother was married and became pregnant by someone other than her husband who was in the army at a base in San Angelo, Texas.

Sadly, I finished this book right after Roe versus Wade was overturned. It's not meant to be a political statement at all. It's meant to be the story that I wish had been my sister's life. It's a story I hope will help birth mothers and fathers realize that every child needs to know their past.

USA Today Best-selling author, Sylvia McDaniel obviously has too much time on her hands. With over eighty western historical and contemporary romance novels, she spends most days torturing her characters. Bad boys deserve punishment and even good girls get into trouble. Always looking for the next plot twist, she's known for her sweet, funny, family-oriented romances.

Married to her best friend for over twenty-five years, they recently moved to the state of Colorado where they like to hike, and enjoy the beauty of the forest behind their home with their spoiled dachshunds Zeus and Bailey. (Zeus has his own column in her newsletter.)

Their grown son, still lives in Texas. An avid football watcher, she loves the Broncos and the Cowboys, especially when they're winning.

www.SylviaMcDaniel.com
Sylvia@SylviaMcDaniel.com
The End!

Made in the USA
Coppell, TX
26 April 2025